HEI

Tamara Hoffa

Erotic Romance

Secret Cravings Publishing
www.secretcravingspublishing.com

A Secret Cravings Publishing Book
Erotic Romance

Hers to Bear
Copyright © 2015 Tamara Hoffa
Print ISBN: 978-1-63105-552-2

First E-book Publication: January 2015

Cover design by Dawné Dominique
Edited by Ariana Gaynor
Proofread by Renee Waring
All cover art and logo copyright © 2015 by Secret Cravings Publishing

ALL RIGHTS RESERVED: This literary work may not be reproduced or transmitted in any form or by any means, including electronic or photographic reproduction, in whole or in part, without express written permission.

All characters and events in this book are fictitious. Any resemblance to actual persons living or dead is strictly coincidental.

PUBLISHER
Secret Cravings Publishing
www.secretcravingspublishing.com

Dedication

Hers to Bear is dedicated to all of the paranormal authors in the world who have given me so many hours of reading enjoyment. I couldn't possibly name them all, but I'd like to mention a few who have touched me greatly. I love humor mixed with shifters and the queens of this, in my opinion are Eve Langlais, Celia Kyle, Shelly Laurenston and Dana Marie Belle. Second are the plot weavers, I envy the evil minds of these Diva's and wish I had their dark and twisted muses, mine is too busy happy dancing to create terrible evil plots! Lol, Carrie Ann Ryan, Laura Kaye, Sherrilyn Kenyon, Lora Leigh, and Jennifer Ashley. There are so many more, but if I named them all it would fill up the whole book!

I hope you enjoy the Animal in Me Series, creating this world was a wonderful journey for me. Bern, the hero in book 1, Hers to Bear is loosely based on my own real life hero, a big, gruff man, with a huge heart, hidden behind a wall of stone, and a hilarious sense of humor. My husband, Michael Hoffa, I love you Pookie Bear.

Happy Reading!

HERS TO BEAR

Tamara Hoffa

Chapter One

Sunlight filtered through the leaves of the maple trees lining Main Street. The light sparkled on the dark red cobblestones, yellow and white sprinkled between dark shadows like stars twinkling in a night sky.

The air was clear and cool, not quite crisp yet, as fall was on the horizon, but had not arrived fully. September brought the promise of autumn leaves blossoming with colors and falling to the ground to be raked into piles for the children to jump and roll around in.

Jenna smiled as she thought about her kindergarten class. She needed to come up with some fun projects to do with the falling leaves. Sarah had been so cute today at nap. She had curled into a little ball when Jenna tried to wake her up and growled at her.

Shifters had "come out" to the human world five years ago, and there was still a lot Jenna didn't know about them, but she was learning more every day. Who would have thought her first teaching job would be at a school where over half the children were shifters?

When she applied for the position in Honey Corners, West Virginia, she hadn't really expected a response. She had heard that shifter communities tended to keep to themselves and rarely hired outsiders. But, less than a month after she sent her resume she received a call asking her to come for an interview, and the rest, as they say, was history.

Honey Corners was a bear shifter community. Mostly grizzly bears and some black bears. There were also a few wolves in town and, surprisingly, a fair number of humans. While many people had been shocked at the great shifter reveal, Jenna wasn't. Maybe it was all the paranormal romances she had been reading for years, but she just accepted the existence of shifters. Secretly, she was titillated by the thought. Often wondering if the stories she'd read held any grains of truth.

Jenna had only moved to Honey Corners three weeks ago. Just in time for the start of the school year. She loved all her students, but the little cubs in her class held a special place in her heart. Maybe she would make some honey cakes for snack tomorrow. The kids and cubs would love that. She had almost everything she needed at home to make them. She could pop into the store and pick up some butter and, of course, some fresh honey.

One of the things Jenna loved about this community was that she didn't feel out of place here. She was a big girl, almost six feet tall and as her momma said, big boned. Which was a nice way of saying fat. She had suffered all through high school and college. Always feeling like a wallflower. Twenty-five years old and she'd never even been kissed. Who wanted to kiss a girl who looked like a football player?

But bears were big. Like really big. All of the male bear shifters she'd met were well over six feet, some were closer to seven feet tall. It was wonderful to actually look up when speaking to someone. Even the women were tall, most close to her height and build. She no longer stuck out like a sore thumb.

Walking down the streets of Honey Corners was like stepping back in time. Quaint shops lined the street, no big box stores here. Family owned businesses were the staple of the community. The shops were neat and clean. Built in an old world style, with gabled roofs and colorful shutters. It reminded her of a picturesque German town.

She passed the bakery and the smell of the fresh baked bread made her mouth water and her stomach grumble. Maybe she'd stop in and pick up a loaf of sour dough on her way home. Still warm from the oven and slathered with melted butter. Her stomach growled again and she placed her hand over it to stifle the noise.

The candy shop was next, and the chocolates in the window were enough to make her roll her eyes in ecstasy. It was a good thing she did a lot of walking or she would gain twenty pounds just from smelling all the food on this street.

Finally Andy's Market came into view. She loved this store. Andy carried everything you could possibly need and more. Most of it locally grown or made. The jams and jellies were to die for, and the honey…well, there were about twenty different kinds and all of the ones she'd tried so far were delicious.

The bell over the door tinkled merrily as she pushed inside. Andy raised his head from the fishing magazine he was reading and waved at her.

"Hi. Miss Jenna."

She loved that he called her by name. She'd lived in Chicago for four years while in college and gone to the same convenience store every day for coffee. In all that time the clerk had never called her by name.

"Hi, Andy. How are you today?"

"Fine, miss, just fine, and you?"

"I'm great, thanks. Just want to pick up some honey."

"Well, you know where it is."

"Yes, I do. Thanks." Jenna headed to the middle of the store and perused the selection. What kind should she choose today? The bell above the door tinkled, but she didn't pay it any attention. Hmm, orange blossom honey, that sounded good. She reached for the jar and a huge paw engulfed her hand as it closed over the container.

"Mine," a gruff voice said, and she looked up and up. No other way to describe it, but a bear of a man stood next to her. At least seven feet tall, with shaggy brown hair and a delicious looking scruff of beard across his chin. Deep brown eyes, like melted chocolate stared into hers with a possessive gaze. Somehow she didn't think it was the honey he was proclaiming ownership of and electric shivers shot down her spine.

* * * *

Bern had come into the store for his daily honey fix. He admitted it, he was addicted to the stuff. He had just bought two dozen biscuits at the bakery and he was going to drown them in honey, along with a nice piece of salmon for dinner.

When he stepped through the door he stopped in his tracks. His nostrils flared and his heart began to race. What was that fabulous scent? Like honey and vanilla, but something else too.

Something that was making his cock stand up and do a happy dance in his pants.

Mate. Oh my God and goddess, his mate was in this store. He couldn't think. Instinct took over and his legs carried him to the source of the tantalizing scent that had his libido raging and his bear roaring.

He was beside her before his brain had caught up with his body. He had to touch her. She was his. His hand covered hers as she reached for a jar of honey on the shelf. "Mine," he growled. When she looked up at him with crystal blue eyes he thought he'd fallen into them and drowned.

Flawless porcelain skin covered a face that could have been painted by Botticelli. Pale blonde lashes framed her startled eyes and her cheeks were flushed an enticing pink. She bit her bottom lip and he wanted to kiss away the sting her torment caused the luscious flesh.

"There's more than one jar," she said, and her voice was husky and sweet.

He released her hand and skimmed his along the velvet softness of her cheek. She shivered.

"I am Bern, and you are mine," he said.

She took a step back and a low growl escaped his throat. His bear didn't like their mate backing away from them.

"I beg your pardon?"

"You are mine. You are my mate."

Fear sparked in the woman. He could scent it, but along with the fear was a slight perfume of desire too. She looked around frantically and Bern could sense she was about to flee. He placed a hand on her arm.

"Do not run from me. Please."

"I need to sit down." She was shaking now.

Bern put his arm around her to steady her. His bear liked that. It wanted their scent to surround her. He started to lead her out of the store.

"Where are you taking me?" She hesitated.

"There is a bench outside where we can sit. It's not far."

She blinked up at him like an owl. "Okay."

Bern led her to the bench and urged her to sit. He knelt down in front of her running a hand over her soft blonde hair. He couldn't stop touching her. She sat, still as a statue, staring at the ground between her feet.

"What is your name, my sweet?"

She looked up like a startled doe. "Jenna Raynes."

He caressed her cheek again. "I am Bern Helms."

"I'm kind of in shock here. I'm your mate? What exactly does that mean? How do you know? I mean, I've read about it in books, but I didn't think it was true."

"It is true, my sweet Jenna. Shifters mate for life. We have one true mate and when we meet, we know immediately. By scent. Instinct. You are mine."

"But, what if I don't want to be? I don't even know you. You could be mean or creepy or a drunk or something."

Bern laughed. "The goddess would not pair us together if we were not meant to be. I assure you I am not a drunk. I rarely drink in fact, and shifters have a very hard time getting drunk anyway, very high metabolism. As for mean or creepy, that you will have to judge for yourself, but my nieces and nephews love me. Children are said to be good judges of character."

"Yes, they are. How many nieces and nephews do you have?"

"Twelve at last count."

"Twelve? Really? How many brothers and sisters do you have?"

"No brothers, five sisters. They are all mated. Perhaps now they will leave me alone. They have been hounding me for years to find a mate."

Jenna laughed, though it sounded a bit forced.

"How about you, my sweet Jenna? Do you have any brothers or sisters?"

"No, I'm an only child. Just me and my parents. They live in Nashville, well a little town outside Nashville."

"What brought you to Honey Corners? You can't have been here long."

"I'm the new kindergarten teacher. I just moved here three weeks ago."

"One of my nieces is in kindergarten. I wonder if she's in your class."

"What's her name?"

"Sarah Keller."

"Sarah is your niece? She is adorable!"

Bern smiled, score one for him, Jenna liked his niece. "She is my sister, Julia's youngest."

Jenna seemed to be relaxing now. She was less stiff and she was smiling. He eased onto the seat beside her and laid his arm along the back of the bench. Jenna leaned into him slightly, he didn't think she realized she did it.

She looked up at him with those incredible eyes and said, "So, what do we do now? I know you sniffed and bam we're mates, but it just doesn't work that way for me."

"We can take it as slow as you need. I'll court you like a human man. We can date, get to know each other, but I warn you my bear is greedy and possessive. He wants you, wants to touch you, kiss you, love you," the last came out as a growl.

A blush flared across her cheeks and the scintillating scent of her desire perfumed the air. He couldn't resist and leaned in for a kiss. He meant it to be just a gentle brush of lips, but the moment his lips touched hers she exhaled a sigh and melted against him.

His tongue slipped inside her mouth to mate with hers, twisting and twining in a dance as old as time. Her arms crept around his neck, toying with the hair that curled at his nape and his bear stretched toward his skin, seeking the feel of his mate's hand.

He pulled her closer, enfolding her in his arms, one hand resting between her shoulder blades and pressing her as close to his chest as possible, the other thrust into the silky mass of her hair, holding her mouth captive for his kiss.

Time stood still as he drank in the taste of his mate. He explored every nook and cranny of her mouth, slid his tongue across her smooth teeth and tender palate. He pulled away and pressed his forehead to hers. His breath came in pants and his cock was hard enough to pound nails.

Jenna was breathing hard too. "Wow," she said.

Yeah, wow. If a kiss could do this to him, what would happen when they made love?

Chapter Two

Bern walked her home and left her at the door with another kiss that curled her toes. Man, she was making up for lost time. That man could kiss like nobody's business. Woo whee!

Jenna toed off her shoes and wandered into the kitchen. She had never gotten the honey, or her bread, but she really needed some coffee. She pulled the bag of coffee beans from the cabinet and measured them into the grinder. The quiet whirl of the machine calmed her rioting nerves. Once the coffee maker was dripping, Jenna stood at the sink and stared at the view outside her kitchen window.

Her little rented house was on the edge of the woods and looking at the quiet beauty usually calmed her down, but at the moment her mind was racing. While, hypothetically she'd dreamed of finding her perfect mate as she read her romance novels, reality was a bit different. Bern seemed nice. God knew he was certainly sexy as hell, but it wasn't instant love. At least not on her side and she didn't think it really was on Bern's side either. A connection, and instant lust, yes, but not love.

Jenna wanted love. There was so much she didn't know about shifters. Which of the tales were true? Did they heal faster? Live longer? Would she age, while Bern stayed young and handsome? That would suck. They really needed to sit down and talk, hopefully at a time when she had her shit together and wasn't feeling like she was on a roller coaster. Maybe she should write down a list of questions. She was a big list girl.

The buzzer on the coffee maker sounded and she poured a cup, adding a generous dollop of creamer and sat down at the kitchen table with a pen and paper. Then a thought struck her. Should she call her mom and dad? Cripes. She'd never had a boyfriend, she didn't know what proper protocol was. Did a mate constitute a boyfriend anyway? Or was it more like a fiancé or a, gulp, husband?

More questions. Alice! She'd call Alice. Her best friend would know what to do. A glance at the clock told her that her friend should be home from work by now, so she pulled the cell phone from her purse and speed dialed.

"What's up girlfriend? How are things in Bear central?"

Thank God for best friends, this was just what she needed.

"Hi. It's so good to hear your voice. I miss you."

"Uh oh, whatza matta?" Alice said, her Chicago accent thick and heavy.

Jenna laughed. "No small talk lead up, huh? You got me already. Well…it's not really a *something wrong,* just kind of a holy crap."

"Spill it, sista. I'm gettin' old here."

"I…kinda…umm…"

"Jenna Marie Raynes!"

"Okay, okay. Put a sock in it. I met my mate today," she squeaked.

"Holy shit!"

"Yeah, that."

"One of those uber sexy bears ya said are all over that weird little town? Damn, I need to move down there, or at least come visit."

"It's not a *weird little town.* I love it here. Stop being such an elitist snob! Miss city girl. Would you really come visit? Damn, I could really use you here right about now."

"Of course, I'll come visit, but I can't come right now. Work is a bitch. Stop trying to steer me off track. Tell me about the bear/man! Is he cute?"

"Cute is not a word I would use to describe Bern."

"Bern, Oh, that's a sexy name. So, dish. I want deets."

Jenna sighed. "He is almost seven feet tall, with big, broad shoulders, and milk chocolate eyes."

"Oh shit, you've got it bad already, don'tcha, girl?"

"I'm afraid I do. That's what I'm worried about."

"Why are you worried? I thought this mate thing was the perfect happily ever after. They mate you. Are always faithful, yadda yadda."

"It is, I guess, but…"

"But what? What is the problem? You said the guy is cute, is he mean or something?"

"No! Bern was very nice, sweet even. It's just…"

Hers to Bear

"For Christ's sake, Jenna, will you just spit it out? You know I love ya, but I haven't got all day here."

"It's a chemical reaction. Pheromones. It's not love," Jenna replied sullenly.

There was a pause on the end of the line and Jenna could just picture Alice pulling the phone away from her face and staring at it. Finally she replied in a surprisingly gentle voice, "Jenna, baby, how do *you* feel about this Bern? Do you think you could love him?"

"Yes," she murmured, in fact she was already falling for the big bear.

"So, what makes you think it's only pheromones on his part? Did you talk to him about it?"

"A little. He said the goddess wouldn't choose us as mates if we weren't meant to be together."

"Damn, that's so sweet I think you gave me a cavity."

"You are such a bitch." Jenna laughed.

"So, what are you going to do now? Fuck like bunnies?"

Jenna could feel her cheeks heat, she cleared her throat. "Umm, yeah, well, that will come, eventually, but Bern said we could take it as slow as I wanted."

"Slow, smoe! Get to the good stuff. Is he *big* all over? Did you check out his package?"

Jenna laughed again. "Well, if the baseball bat that was pressing into my thigh when he kissed me was any indication, I might not walk for a week afterward."

"Damn skippy! That's what I'm talkin' 'bout. You get you some of that. It'll fix you right up."

"Alice Louise Miller, I'm gonna tell your mother on you!"

"Shit, Momma would tell you the same."

They both laughed because it was true, Mary Jenkins was a wild woman. Since her husband had passed, she had a string of boyfriends a mile long. They all wore broad smiles from her ardent attentions.

"Listen, girl," Alice said, a serious note in her voice. "This is what you've been waiting for your whole life. Don't fuck it up by overthinking it. Give the guy a chance. Give yourself a chance."

"Thanks. I knew I could count on you. I wish you were here."

"Hey, you know I'm only a phone call away, and if I need to hop on a plane and kick some bear ass, you know I will."

"Yeah, I know you will, but I'm not so sure even *you* could kick this bear's ass."

"I'll bring my Louisville Slugger. Me and Louis can take care of any problem, together."

"I love you, Al."

"I love you too, Jen. I expect daily reports."

"Daily?"

"Well, maybe not daily, but every few days at least."

"Okay, I promise I'll keep in touch. Thanks for listening."

"Anytime."

"Oh, one more thing, do you think I should tell my folks?"

Alice was quiet for a few minutes. "No, not yet. I'd wait until you're sure everything is going to work out and then tell them."

"That's what I thought too. Thanks."

"Don't do anything I wouldn't do."

"Well, that leaves just about everything open."

"That's the idea!" Alice replied with a laugh.

* * * *

Moments after Bern dropped Jenna at her door he was on the phone. There were things he had neglected to tell his erstwhile mate. He was the *Sippe Leiter* of Honey Corners, the Clan leader. That meant as his mate there would be those who would try to use her as a pawn in the game of shifter politics. He would have to put a guard on her, and he had a feeling his feisty little mate wouldn't like that idea one bit.

Martin, his second, answered the phone on the first ring. "*Ja,* Bern?"

"Call the *Sippe*. Meeting. My house. Twenty minutes."

"Yes, sir. Is something wrong?"

A smile spread across Bern's face and he breathed in deeply, enjoying the residual scent of his mate. "No, my friend, nothing is wrong. Something is right. Very right."

"Are you drunk, Bern?"

"Ha ha. No…I have met my mate." Bern held the phone away from his ear in anticipation of the explosion to come.

"Woo Hoo! Holy Fucking Hell! About God damn time!"

"I thought you would be pleased."

"Pleased? I'm fucking overjoyed! Who is she? Do I know her? Is she a grizzly?"

"Slow down, my friend. Her name is Jenna, she's new in town. Human. I don't know if you've met her."

"Human? The hot little school teacher?"

Bern growled.

"Sorry, boss. I was part of the committee that interviewed her for the post at the school. She is…"

"You best not finish that sentence, Martin, if you wish to keep your balls attached to your body."

"Yes, sir. Oh, shit. She's human. Have you marked her? She'll need a guard."

"Precisely why I'm calling the meeting. You best get off the phone with me and get to making those calls."

"Are you kidding me? All I have to do is call your sisters and the whole clan will know in a micro-second." Martin chortled.

Bern joined in the laughter, his heart lighter than it had been in years. "That's true. I'll be sure to cover my ears. I imagine their squeals will be heard all the way to Asheville."

"Asheville, hell, my bet's on Nashville, maybe even Dallas, Texas!"

Bern rolled his eyes at his second's good natured ribbing and hung up the phone without bothering to say goodbye. He was almost home and he had a lot to do before the *Sippe* arrived. The Tudor style home sat atop a large hill overlooking most of the town. It was the seat of power. The woods surrounded the back of the property, and a nice stream, teaming with fish ran nearby. His bear loved the easy access to hunting and fishing the property provided. The human loved the solitude of the hundred-plus acres that kept the *Sippe Leiter* safe and secure.

What would his new mate think of his den? It was family property, passed down from generation to generation. He had lived there all his life. His grandparents had built the original house and his parents had added onto it over the years. Now, it was a sprawling monstrosity. Empty and hollow, with children no longer filling the halls and rooms.

He couldn't wait to fill it with life again.

Stained glass filled the top of the heavy oak door, casting brilliant patterns of color across the hardwood floors in the foyer. Bern stepped into the cool, dark interior. The ceiling stretched the entire length of the two stories throughout the entranceway and the living room, dormer windows allowed natural sunlight to filter into the area, giving it an open and inviting feel.

Exposed beams, crisscrossed the pale white stucco with deep chocolate. The staircase to the second floor was all hand turned oak planks his father had lovingly shaped and the banister was a work of art. Elaborate carvings of forest animals, with a bear's head at each end. A *Sippe* member had created the masterpiece.

Bern's mother, Marta, had loved to cook. One of the last things his father had done for her, before the accident that took their lives, was to modernize the kitchen. Stainless steel gleamed amidst the granite countertops. Everything was top of the line, from the ceramic cooktop to the built-in double ovens and duel refrigerators. A kitchen made for entertaining large groups of hungry bears.

He briefly wondered if Jenna liked to cook, and then dismissed the thought. He didn't care. He could always hire someone if she didn't. He had a mate. Such a simple and complex thing. His joy knew no bounds, but he was overcome with fear too. Jenna would be a target. He needed to keep her safe above all else.

Pulling a bottle of water from the fridge, he downed half the contents in a single gulp. His mind already formulating his strategy. The front door flew open with such force he was surprised the glass didn't shatter and the excited voices of his sisters all calling at once assaulted his ears.

"In the kitchen," he called, and was immediately surrounded by too many arms and mouths to sort out. All hugging and kissing and talking at once.

"Oh, Bern, I'm so happy for you."

"I can't wait to meet her."

"Is she pretty?"

"Is she here?"

"Have you marked her yet?"

Bern took a step back from the women and held his hands up in a gesture to stop.

"Hello, sisters. It's so nice to see you too." He laughed.

Julia looked sheepish, "Sorry, Bern. Hi." She waved her fingers.

The rest of the women stood in various poses of demand, hands on hips or crossed over their chests and big sister looks firmly in place.

Keeping his hands out in a placating gesture he said. "I know you want answers, but I don't want to go through all of this twice. You're just going to have to wait until the rest of the *Sippe* gets here and listen with everyone else."

"That's not fair." Dagmar stomped. "We're your sisters, we should get to hear first."

"Suck it up, buttercup," he said, giving her the standard response they'd used since they were children.

She crossed her arms and turned her back to him, and he snuck up behind her and kissed her cheek.

"I love you, sissy."

Dagmar threw her arms around his neck and hugged him tight. "I love you too, bud."

Sometimes sisters were easy. A kiss and an "I love you" made everything better. "Let's move this party into the living room. Everyone should be arriving soon."

A knock sounded at the door before the words had even left his mouth. Martin was the first to arrive, followed by a steady stream of clan members. The Honey Corner's *Sippe* was large, with nearly four-hundred members. Not all would attend the meeting, of course, but the heads of the families would all be here.

The house was large, but not big enough to accommodate all the bears that showed up for this auspicious occasion. So, the proceedings were moved outside.

As more people arrived, small clusters of family and friends dotted the landscape of the back lawn. Four barbeque grills were heated and every kind of meat was cooking, chicken, fish, steak, hot dogs and hamburgers. Beer and soft drinks were passed around and the conversations were buzzing with speculation.

"What is going on?"

"Why has Bern called this impromptu meeting?"

"Is something wrong?"

Bern stepped from the shadows and walked to the center of the "circle." Everyone fell silent and all heads bowed in respect to their leader. "Goddess be with you," Bern intoned in a booming voice.

"Brotherhood, strength and honor hold the circle," cheered the group.

Bern smiled broadly and made eye contact with each bear in the circle, nodding in acknowledgement as he made his way around the gathering. Before he had made it even half-way 'round someone in the crowd yelled out. "What's going on *Sippe Leiter*? You're smiling, so I'm guessing we aren't going to war."

Bern threw back his head and laughed. "No, we are not going to war. At least not yet, I hope. I have news to share with you, my clan. Grand news."

Dagmar, never one to let her brother get away with anything, yelled out. "Will you stop dicking around and just tell them brother!"

A collective gasp came from the crowd, but Bern only laughed again.

"Yes, sweet *schwester*, I will quit dicking around and tell them. I have met my mate!"

A cacophony of whoops, cheers and hollers threatened to cause a rock slide in the surrounding mountains. Bern was engulfed by too many arms to count, slapping him on the back, shoving his shoulders, giving him awkward man hugs, the women kissed his cheeks, the older ones patting his head and said, "It's about time."

When the hoopla finally began to die down, Bern raised his arms to call for silence. "Hold, my friends. My mate, Jenna, is human. Until I am able to change her, she will be at risk. I need you all to be on guard. I will be assigning guards to my Jenna, but she doesn't know my position in the clan or the danger she is in. So, you will need to be discrete."

"The wolves may also think this is an opportunity to attack, thinking I may be distracted from my duties. This is a time of great joy for me and our clan, but it is also a dangerous time. We must be on the alert, ever vigilant and attentive."

Nods of assent greeted Bern's pronouncement. "Let's eat!" he said, and left the center of the circle to mingle with the crowd. Bern spent the evening eating and drinking with his friends and family, but his sweet Jenna was never far from his mind. The scent of his mate overpowered the smell of the cooking food.

The sweet smells of the forest night couldn't eclipse her honey scent from his nostrils. He wanted to go to her, to hold her in his arms again, and kiss her ruby lips. To bury his head in the crook of her neck and breathe in her delicious aroma, to bathe in it, until their scents merged into one.

His cock was a hard throbbing ache in his pants. How was he going to stay away from her? He promised her he would take it as slowly as she wanted, but right now he was ready to kick his own ass for saying that. He wanted her, and he didn't want to wait. Oh, God, his balls were already turning blue.

Bern slipped into the house and went to his office. He poured himself a glass of orange juice and turned on his computer. Feeling a bit like a stalker, he opened Facebook and did a search for Jenna Raynes.

He found her easily enough, and sent her a friend request. It was only a moment and his request was accepted. It seemed Jenna was online. The chat window opened in the corner of his screen.

Hi

Hi, what are you doing?

Talking to you.

Funny.

I'm taking a bath

Bern groaned and rubbed his throbbing crotch.

Oh my God, you are so mean. Can I come join you?

There was a long pause.

Are you there? Bern asked

Yes, I'm here. I just didn't really know how to answer that.

Honestly.

Well, honestly, part of me would like you to join me, but I don't think I'm ready for that yet.

You're killing me here. You are all I can think about.

I've been thinking about you too.

What have you been thinking?

I'm not telling.

Why not?

A girl has to have some mystery.

You're no fun.

I may be more fun than you can handle.

I'd like to try.

I think this conversation is getting dangerous.

I like danger, how about you?

No. I am a play it safe kind of girl

I bet I can lure you to the wild side.

That's what I'm afraid of. My water is getting cold and my face is getting hot. I'm going to say goodnight.

Scaredy cat

Meow

The green light next to Jenna's name went out, signifying that she had signed off of Facebook. Bern spent a few minutes looking at Jenna's profile. She liked Country music that was good, they had that in common. Their tastes in movies and books were similar.

He looked through her pictures and was enchanted by the images of his mate. She was so full of life, always smiling and laughing. There were many pictures of her mother and father, and several with a lovely young woman, tagged as Alice. Those two looked like trouble together.

Funny, there weren't any pictures of his mate with other men. Bern was glad because he would have wanted to rip their heads off, but he couldn't understand how his beautiful mate hadn't been surrounded by suitors.

A knock sounded at the door to his office and Martin opened the door without waiting for a reply.

"We've got trouble, the west quadrant boundaries have been breached."

Bern bolted to his feet. "Is Jenna safe?"

"Your Mate is fine. Hans is on guard duty and reports all is well."

"Have the sentries apprehended the trespasser?"

"Yes. A young wolf. I think it might just be a case of adolescent ignorance or curiosity."

"Okay, bring the wolf here and let me speak with him. If that is the case, I will contact Bastian and let him deal with the miscreant."

Martin nodded and backed out the door. Bern ran his fingers through his unruly hair and prayed this was only a mistake and not an effort to invade his territory. He didn't want to deal with the wolves right now. He had a mate to court.

Chapter Three

Jenna smiled as she slipped from her bath and wrapped herself in a fluffy bath sheet. She cleared the steam from the mirror and gazed at her reflection. Did she look different? Her face was flushed with color, more from Bern's suggestive words than the heat of her bath. Her eyes were bright and shining, and she looked...happy. It's not that she had been unhappy with her life before meeting Bern. She loved her job and her little house, but she *had* been lonely.

Moving away from her family and friends had been hard, but even when she had lived at home a part of her was always lonely. Her longing for someone special to love made her feel alone even in a crowded room. Now, she felt different. She felt *hope*, for the first time in ages. Hope that a chubby girl from Nashville could actually find love.

She still had her doubts about the mating, but anticipation and joy filled her soul. She pulled her sexiest nightgown from a drawer, and let the silky material caress her body as she slipped it on. Everything felt more intense tonight. The glide of the silk against her thighs as she climbed between her cool crisp sheets was decadent. The moonlight filtering through her lace curtains bathed the room in soft white light. She turned off her bedside lamp and snuggled deep into her down cocoon. To sleep, perchance to dream, she thought as she drifted into darkness.

The horrible blaring of her alarm clock jolted Jenna awake. She usually awoke before the damn thing went off. God, what an annoying noise. She slammed her hand onto the button on the top of the clock to still the racket and pushed the covers back, swinging her legs over the side of the bed.

She yawned and stretched. What a wonderful morning. She had slept like the dead. Sliding the button on the alarm clock to off, so it wouldn't go off again, she headed to the bathroom. After taking care of business, brushing her teeth and quickly French braiding her hair, she returned to the bedroom and dressed.

It was a school day, she chose soft black slacks and a colorful peasant blouse. The kids loved bright colors and so did Jenna. She slipped a pair of espadrilles on and headed for the kitchen and coffee. The elixir of the gods.

Jenna sipped her coffee and nibbled on a bagel while she checked her e-mails and Facebook. Nothing interesting there. Her e-mails were mostly spam. How did these people get her e-mail address? No, she certainly didn't want a bigger penis, or bigger boobs. Hers were too big already, she laughed.

Jenna finished her coffee and put the plate from her bagel in the dishwasher. Dropping her phone in her purse she grabbed her large tote bag with her lesson planner and all her teacher trappings and headed out the door.

It was a beautiful fall morning, and Jenna took a deep breath of the crisp air as she stepped off the porch. There was a faint sent of burning leaves on the breeze and a pair of birds in a nearby maple tree seemed to chirp "hello" when she passed.

Her long legged stride carried her swiftly toward her destination. The school was only six blocks away and she loved making the walk each morning. When winter came and snow covered the ground she might have to drive, but for now she would enjoy the weather and the exercise she so desperately needed.

About two blocks into her walk she began to feel a funny prickling on her neck. That creepy feeling you get when someone is watching you. She rubbed the back of her neck and glanced surreptitiously around. No one.

Quit acting like a ninny.

An older man and woman sat in rocking chairs on their front porch and she waved as she passed them, they nodded in acknowledgment. Jenna looked around again, she could see no one, but the couple on the porch and they weren't watching her. Why did she feel eyes on her?

It might be paranoia, but she quickened her pace anyway. She wanted off the street, and into the relative safety of her classroom.

Jenna rushed through the front door of the school and sighed in relief. God, that was strange. What was the matter with her this morning? She chuckled at her own foolishness and made a beeline for her classroom. The kids would be arriving soon and she needed to make sure everything was set up for the day.

Once the classroom filled with children Jenna was too busy to obsess over her feeling of being watched, but at recess the feeling returned. She sat on a bench in the shade, talking with one of the other teachers, but once again had the uncomfortable feeling of being watched.

When the bell rang at three o'clock and all the children fled like the tide rushing out to sea, Jenna sat at her desk and rubbed the back of her neck. She was reluctant to make the walk home. What was she going to do? She could call a cab, but that just seemed stupid. She wasn't even sure they had cabs in Honey Corners.

As she pondered her predicament, a knock sounded on her doorframe. She looked up to see her bear filling the doorway. Relief coursed through her veins. Bern was here. She was safe.

"Hi," she said. "Come in. I'm so happy to see you." Jenna rose from the desk and practically threw herself into Bern's arms.

He held her close and nuzzled her neck. "Not that I'm not happy for the welcome, but is something wrong?"

Jenna leaned back in his arms and looked up into his chocolate eyes. "I'm sorry. I've had a strange day."

Bern's forehead crinkled in concern. "How so?"

"It's silly, really. Don't worry about it. I'm just glad you're here."

"Nothing you feel is silly, Mate. Tell me. What troubles you?"

"I've just had this creepy feeling all day that someone is watching me."

An odd look flashed across Bern's features, but was gone before she could identify it.

"I'm sure it's nothing to be concerned about. I came to walk you home. I hope that's all right?"

"It's wonderful! Just let me pack up my stuff and lock up the classroom and we can be on our way."

Before she could pull out of his arms Bern leaned down and stole a kiss. It was only a brief brushing of the lips, but Jenna felt it all the way to her toes. An electric jolt of energy that made her tingle all over and her pussy cream. God that man could kiss.

Bern insisted on carrying her tote bag. He should have looked silly, but nothing could diminish his masculine appeal, at least not in Jenna's eyes. She locked the classroom door and Bern enfolded her under his free arm. What a strange sensation, she felt so small and feminine tucked into his side.

He smiled down at her and her heart skipped a beat, so handsome, and he looked at her like she hung the moon. Damn she could really get used to this. They stepped into the afternoon sunshine and Jenna tipped her head back and took a deep breath. The golden light and warmth lifted the last of the stress from her shoulders.

"Where would you like to go for dinner?" Bern asked.

Jenna felt a blush crawl across her cheeks, but she boldly suggested, "Why don't we stop by the market on the way home and I could cook for you instead." There were two reason's Jenna didn't want to go out, well maybe three. She really wanted to be able to talk to Bern without worrying about anyone overhearing. She didn't want people watching her, she'd had that feeling of being watched all day and if she was in some fancy restaurant with this handsome man, everyone would stare. Wondering what he could possibly see in her. And last, but not least, she wanted more of those kisses…maybe even more than kisses.

"Are you sure? I'd love to take you out."

Jenna looked at the sidewalk, she was so bad at this. "Yes, I'm sure," she mumbled.

Bern stopped and placed his big paw under her chin, he tipped her face up, so she met his gaze.

"What is it, my mate? Why are you looking so shy?"

"I'm just not good at this dating stuff." She shrugged. "If you want to go out, that's fine."

"That's not what I said, little one. I only want to spend time with you. Where matters not. If you want to eat at your home, that is fine. Let's go to Andy's and see what looks good."

"I was thinking, if you don't mind that is, maybe you could grill a nice salmon filet on the deck. I could make a salad and bake some potatoes. I was going to make some honey cakes too."

Bern's eyes sparkled at the mention of honey cakes, these bears all had such sweet tooth's. "Honey cakes? How could a bear say no to that?"

Jenna nudged him with her shoulder. "Is that the only part you heard?"

"No, I heard every word, my mate. Salmon sounds wonderful." He squeezed her shoulder and picked up the pace, walking briskly in the direction of the market.

* * * *

Bern breathed in the scent of his mate. Jenna wanted to talk about food and the only thing he could think of was eating *her* up. Her scent was driving him mad, honey, vanilla and something else, uniquely Jenna's. His dick was so hard he could barely walk. He tried everything to calm his raging libido, but nothing worked. He'd recited the multiplication table, baseball statistics, he'd even tried to picture his grandmother in a nightgown. Nothing worked. Now, his beautiful mate wanted to spend the evening in her den. No people around to help him maintain control. How the hell was he going to make it through the night without marking and mating her? His bear was pacing and growling in his head. *Mine, mine, mate, mark.* Patience my friend. He tried to calm his bear, but it was a lost cause. Until Jenna was marked as theirs, his bear would be on edge.

The bell above the door on Andy's dinged as they stepped inside. Bern's nostrils flared as he took in the scents of the store. There were two unmated male bears inside, but what had his bear growling was the scent of wolf. He knew the scent of every shifter who lived in Honey Corners and this was not a resident.

Bern dropped his arm from around his mate's shoulder and took her hand. He tugged slightly, drawing her behind his bulk. Jenna placed her small hand on his waist and tried to lean around him.

"Stay," he growled, his bear close to the surface. Bern could smell the sour stench of fear roll off his mate.

"What's the matter? What's wrong?"

"Maybe nothing, but there is a wolf in the store."

Jenna stopped and he glanced over his shoulder to find her standing with her hands on her hips.

"What is your problem? Are you some kind of speciest? There are wolves all over town."

"This wolf is not from town," he hissed.

"So, what? I don't understand what the problem is."

"No, you don't. I will explain later. For now just please stay behind me."

Andy stepped out of the back room and up to the checkout counter. His eyes widened at the sight of Jenna and Bern together, than a frown creased his brow. "Bring Jenna here Bern. I will keep her safe while you deal with the intruder."

Bern nodded and pulled Jenna behind him as he walked behind the counter. His bear didn't want to let her go, but he trusted Andy to keep her safe. He looked the other bear straight in the eye. "She is mine," he growled. Jenna huffed behind him. "Guard her as if you were guarding me."

Andy bowed his head and tipped it to the left, exposing his neck. "*Ja, Sippe Leiter.*"

A mixture of confusion, fear and anger radiated from his mate. He was going to have a lot of explaining to do. Placing his finger to his lips in a gesture to be quiet, he turned from the pair and stalked into the aisles.

He followed the wolf's scent to the back of the store. Tall for a wolf, he stood in human form in front of the meat refrigerator. Shaggy multi-colored brown and blond hair fell to his shoulders, concealing his face as he leaned over the meat case.

The wolf had to know that Bern approached, but he didn't turn or lift his head. What the hell was going on here? Bern walked to side of the wolf and he finally stood and turned to face Bern.

"Greetings, *Sippe Leiter*, from Von Drake."

Aha, so this wolf had come to deliver a message.

"If you had news for me you should have made an appointment. Not be skulking around in this store."

"My apologies, *Sippe Leiter*, I meant to call on you upon leaving the store. I did not know I would meet you here."

Bern couldn't hold back the growl that rumbled in his throat. "Speak. What message do you have for me?"

"Von Drake wishes to extend his congratulation to you on meeting your mate. He wants you to know that he considers the mate bond sacred and will not interfere."

Bern's bear did not like this wolf, he smelled a lie on him. He couldn't tell if it was the wolf in front of him who lied, or if the lie was being reiterated from the Wolf alpha. However, politics dictated he at least pretend to accept the wolf's congratulations.

"Please tell Von Drake I appreciate his good wishes."

The wolf reached into his back pocket and removed an envelope. "An invitation for you and your mate, *Sippe*." The wolf nodded and backed away. "I will take my leave now." The wolf continued to back away, never turning his back to Bern. Once through the front door he shifted to his wolf form and took off at a full run.

How the hell had the wolf made it past the guards at the clan border without detection? Bern was not a happy bear. He turned the heavily embossed envelope in his hand, and broke the wax seal. Jenna and Andy came up to his side. "What's that?" Jenna asked.

"An invitation, apparently." He pulled a sheet of stationary from the envelope, and unfolded a hand-written note.

> *The honor of your presence is requested at a formal dinner*
> *Saturday, September 26, 2014*
> *6:30 pm*
> *1239 Von Drake Place*
> *Wolvesberg*
> *R.S.V.P.*
> *555-629-6034*

Oh man, Martin was going to have a coronary when he heard about this, but how could he say no? It would be an insult to the alpha of the wolf pack.

A million thoughts raced through Bern's mind, but first and foremost was the safety of his clan. He needed to call Martin, but the soft hand of his mate rested on his arm. He looked down into her confused eyes. "I'm sorry, little one. I promise I will explain all this when we get back to your house. I must make a call now. Why don't you get the things we need for dinner. Andy will help you." He lifted her hand from his arm and kissed her palm, and then placed her hand on Andy's arm.

"Come, sweet Jenna, tell me what delicacies you seek for your dinner this evening," Andy said with his easy smile as he led her away.

Jenna looked back over her shoulder at Bern, but allowed herself to be directed to picking out the salmon and the rest of the ingredients for dinner.

Bern speed dialed Martin and he picked up on the first ring.

"*Ja, Sippe.*"

"I just had a visitor at Andy's market."

"Oh?"

"*Ja.* Somehow a Von Drake wolf made it past all the guards, without notice, to deliver an invitation to my mate and me. Make sure he has left clan lands."

"Was it a threat sir?"

"No, simply an invitation to dinner. However, Von Drake knows of my mating already. How, I do not know. That makes me nervous. And the fact that this wolf made it past our guards undetected…that is unacceptable."

"I agree, sir. I am sorry." Bern could hear the contrition in his second's voice. "I will see to it."

"I know you will. I will be with my mate tonight. I do not wish to be disturbed unless it is an emergency. Do you understand?"

"Yes, sir."

"Good." Bern hung up without further discussion and went in search of his mate. He found her at the register checking out with her purchases. Wonderful timing. He snuck up behind her and wrapped his arms around her waist, nuzzling her neck and kissing the sweet smelling spot behind her ear. Jenna shivered and he licked the shell of her ear and whispered, "You taste like honey."

A delicate blush crawled across her cheeks and Bern leaned in and brushed his cheek against hers. He wanted to feel her warmth against his flesh. Her skin was soft as eider down and he closed his eyes in bliss. His mate. God the peace of touching his mate.

Jenna giggled and it pulled him from his trance. "That tickles," she said.

Bern waggled his eyebrows and Jenna laughed, a deep rich sound that grabbed him by the balls and pulled. He couldn't resist and turned her in his arms, pulling her in for a blistering kiss.

Jenna melted into him, her arms going around his neck. She stretched up on her tip toes and molded her entire body to his. Her breasts pressed into his chest, his throbbing erection pressed into the tender swell of her belly, and it was all he could do not to grind against her. God his mate was perfection. He needed to get her out of here and somewhere private. He slowly gentled the kiss and used every ounce of willpower he possessed to pull back. Now was not the time or place to ravish his mate.

Andy cleared his throat, "That will be thirty-five dollars and forty-two cents."

Jenna started to open her purse, but Bern stayed her hand. "Here you go." He handed Andy a fifty dollar bill and picked up the two bags, "Keep the change, my friend." He put his arm around Jenna and led her from the store. "Come, little one, let's go home."

* * * *

A thousand thoughts ran through Jenna's mind as they stepped out onto the street. What in the hell was with everyone calling Bern *Sippe*? What did that mean? Who was Von Drake, and why would he want them to come to dinner? Why did it matter that there was a wolf in Andy's store? There where wolves all over town. Bern had some explaining to do and he'd better get to it or he was going to see one pissed off Jenna.

"I can see the wheels turning in your head, my mate. I promise I will explain when we get home, but it is complicated and I don't want to get into it on the street."

"Am I that transparent?"

Bern crooked a brow, "No, my mate, but I can feel your anxiety and smell the burning of your anger."

"You can smell my anger? That's kind of creepy. And what do you mean you can feel my anxiety? How?"

"While we are not mate bonded, yet. My bear knows you as his mate and when we are this close he can sense your feelings. Once we are fully mated I will be able to sense your feelings even when we are apart."

"Seriously? I'm not sure I like that idea. I won't have any privacy."

"You will be able to sense my feeling too. It is a wonderful feeling of closeness. My parents often shared tender looks from across the room that shut out everyone else. I can't wait to experience that myself."

"Your parents are gone?"

Sadness colored Bern's features, "Yes, Four years now. They passed together in a train accident in Prague."

"I'm sorry. I didn't mean to bring up bad memories."

"It's all right, little one. They are not bad memories. I mourn their passing, but I have only fond memories of my parents. They were wonderful people, wonderful parents. They loved us well. They are remembered with love." He kissed her on the forehead. "Tell me about your parents."

"My dad is a bank examiner and my mom is a stay at home mom. Unusual I know in this day and age, but she loves it. She likes to garden and grows beautiful roses and orchids. Dad built her a green house. They live in a little town about forty miles west of Nashville on five acres of land. Daddy works in Nashville, mostly. Although he travels to some of the surrounding area banks too."

"Are you close to them?"

"Yes, we're very close. I lived at home until college. They weren't happy at all when I chose to go away for school. They wanted me to go to MTSU and stay at home, but I needed to branch out on my own."

"What did they think about your moving to Honey Corners?"

"They weren't happy that I decided to settle someplace other than Tennessee, but at least West Virginia isn't too far away and they can visit easily enough. They plan to come for Christmas."

"Good. I can't wait to meet them."

Jenna felt her cheeks heat, she'd never had a boyfriend to introduce to her parents. What would they think of Bern? He was so handsome. Would they wonder what a man like him saw in a girl like her?

"What is that look for?"

"What look?"

"You're blushing."

"I've never had a boyfriend before."

"I think perhaps then all the men you have met before have been blind and stupid, but I am glad they were because it saves me from having to hunt them down and kill them." Bern growled.

Jenna stopped dead in her tracks and gazed up at him in stunned silence. He was serious. Bern shrugged his shoulders and planted a kiss on the end of her nose. "I cannot help it. I am a jealous man."

They continued walking in companionable silence and reached Jenna's house in a few minutes. She unlocked the front door and Bern held her back from entering. "Let me check the house first please."

He left her standing on the front porch while he took the bags into the house. She saw the lights flip on methodically throughout the rooms and then Bern returned to the porch. "All clear," he said and pulled her into the house. He attempted to pin her against the wall and kiss her senseless, but Jenna put her hands on his chest and pushed. It was like pushing against a brick wall!

"Oh no you don't, Mr. Bear. This honeycomb is closed until I get some answers. Get your furry butt to the kitchen and you can talk while I make dinner. I want to know what the hell is going on around here."

Bern had the good grace to look sheepish. "Yes, ma'am," he said and strode toward the kitchen, leaving Jenna to follow that delectable and at the moment, not in the least bit furry backside. *Oh yum.*

Jenna pointed to a kitchen chair. "Sit. Talk."

"Okay, little one. Don't get your panties in a bunch. I promised I would tell you everything and I will. What do you want to know first?"

"What is this '*Sippe*' business, and why did Andy act so weird around you?"

"You would ask the hardest question first," Bern mumbled.

Jenna arched a brow at him.

"Sorry, I was hoping we could start with something less intimidating, but we may as well get right to it. *Sippe Leiter* is my title. It loosely translates to clan leader."

Jenna's mouth fell open.

"Y-y-you're the clan leader? Head bear? *Numero uno*? Head honcho? Big Kahuna?"

It was pretty funny to see a seven foot grizzly blush, but Bern did, all the way to the tips of his ears. "Um, yeah."

Jenna flopped into a chair across from him. "Wow. Shit. So, if I mate with you I'll be like the first lady, or some such shit?"

Bern growled. "There is no if, you are my mate."

Anger burned in Jenna's chest. "You better slow your roll, mister. That crap might work on bears, but I'm a human. *I* get to choose who I *mate*. Not fate and not *you*!"

Bern took a deep breath and she watched as his fists clenched and unclenched at his sides. Sadness washed over his features and his entire body stiffened. "You are quite right, little one. I apologize. It is your choice, but you must understand how I feel. I have waited for you for over two hundred years. Finding you is a dream come true for me. If you reject me, it is likely I will die of a broken heart."

Jenna gasped in shock because the look on Bern's face said he was not being melodramatic, he was serious. He looked so forlorn and so alone, she went to him and dropped to her knees on the floor in front of his chair. She threw her arms around his waist and hugged him tight. Bern's hand gently stroked her hair and then slid under her chin to tilt her head up until she was looking into his eyes.

Chapter Four

Jenna's beautiful blue eyes gazed up at him swimming with unshed tears. He reached down and pulled her onto his lap, kissing her eyelids, temples, cheeks, and then down to the corners of her mouth. He teased and coaxed at her lips until they opened for him like a flower to the sun and dipped inside to taste her honey sweetness. God, she was exquisite.

One hand held tight to the braid in her hair while the other roamed her back, pulling her ever closer as his mouth plundered the depths of hers. He could feel her nipples peak against his chest and smell the scent of her desire.

A small moan escaped her lips and Jenna tugged his shirt loose from the waist of his pants so she could slip her soft hands underneath. Bern could not stop the growl from his bear at the feel of her running her hands over his chest.

He reached behind and pulled his shirt off with one hand, giving her free access to his upper body. Jenna purred in appreciation at the revelation and Bern preened with pride. Jenna kissed down the side of his neck to his chest and swirled her tongue around one of his nipples. The flat brown disc stood up in notice, and an electric jolt shot straight to Bern's cock.

Bern kissed Jenna's neck, the delicate spot just behind her ear made her shiver. He continued down, pushing the collar of her peasant blouse off her shoulder and baring her lacey bra. The swell of her breast above the cup received the same treatment, and then he used his teeth to lower the cup and expose her beautiful flesh.

He licked the strawberry nipple and then drew it into his mouth and sucked. Jenna bucked so hard she almost fell off his lap. "Oh my God. That feels so good," she murmured.

"Maybe we should move somewhere more comfortable?" Bern said pulling back to look deeply into her eyes.

Jenna stared at him for a long moment, finally she nodded. "Yes, let's go to my bedroom."

Bern was surprised. He had been thinking of the couch in the living room. He didn't think Jenna was ready for a full mating, but his little mate was constantly surprising him. "Are you sure, little one?"

"I'm sure. Just…remember I've never done this before." She licked her lips.

"Oh, my sweet Jenna, that's something I would never forget. I am so honored to be your first. I promise I will make it good for you." He leaned in and gave her a kiss full of all the passion and love that was filling his heart.

Bern stood with her in his arms, never breaking the kiss and carried her to the bedroom. He kicked the bedroom door closed with his foot and didn't bother to turn on any lights. It wasn't fully dark outside yet. So, the room was lit by the twilight.

Jenna's bedroom was like her, bright and colorful. Feminine and sweet. A queen size bed sat against the far wall covered in a quilt of greens and blues, cherry night stands sat on either side of the bed. Two bookcases overflowing with romance novels took up one wall and a small dressing table with a blue stool graced the side of the room. Throw pillows of every color of the rainbow adorned the top of the bed.

Bern allowed Jenna to slowly slide down his body until her feet touched the floor. He pulled the tie from her braid and ran his fingers through her hair, spilling the thick tresses over her shoulders and then he proceeded to gently peel off her clothing one item at a time. He wanted to worship his mate. He removed her blouse and bra, caressing her shoulders and neck, kissing and touching, trying to keep her nerves from overrunning her desire.

He dropped to his knees and removed her shoes. Her cute little toes were painted pink and he had to kiss each one. He slid his hands up her calves and over her thick thighs, he had to stop there to squeeze, oh God, those thighs, what they did to him, and then her luscious ass. He couldn't wait to see that ass. His hands slipped around to the front and he undid the button on her trousers, sliding down the zipper, he pushed her slacks and underwear to her ankles.

Bern leaned in and kissed her stomach and Jenna trembled. He rested his head against her middle and just held her close for a moment. She sifted her finger through his hair and sighed. Bern looked up and smiled at her. "Step out of these for me, little one."

Jenna complied stepping out of her garments and taking a step back at the same time, this caused Bern's hands to slip from her waist to her ass and he left them there, crawling forward on his knees he nuzzled at her mound and Jenna gasped.

"Open for me, baby," he said and he moved his hands to the back of her thighs and applied pressure to spread her legs apart.

Jenna widened her stance and Bern kissed the curls at the juncture of her thighs. He darted his tongue out and swiped it across her opening. *Damn, she tastes good.* He took a long lick from the bottom of her slit to the top and then swirled his tongue around her clit and Jenna shuddered.

"Oh my God, Bern."

"Feel good, baby?"

"Mm, yeah. Do that again."

Bern chuckled. He used a finger to tease her slit, back and forth, back and forth and slowly dipped it inside. All the while licking and sucking her clit. Jenna was moaning now, thrusting her hips in time to the movement of his finger. He added a second finger and her moans turned to chanting his name. Her cream was coating his hand and his tongue. His dick was so hard, he was about to cum in his pants like a randy teenager. She tasted like heaven, like nothing and no one else in the world. His mate. His life.

She was panting now. Calling his name. He added a third finger and bit down on her clit. She came screaming his name. His arm around her waist was the only thing that kept her upright. Bern slowly brought her down from her climax. Making sure she got every moment of pleasure possible and then he lowered her to the bed and lay down beside her. Cupping her face and kissing her deeply, his hands thrust into her hair, holding her head in place for his kiss.

When he pulled back she looked at him with passion glazed eyes. "You are beautiful when you come, little one," he said.

Jenna blushed all the way to her pretty pink nipples. "Thank you, I think. But, what about you? You didn't come."

"We're not finished my pet. We've only barely started."

"Oh." Jenna laughed and turned to snuggle into his side. "Then I guess it's my turn to play," she said as she began to run her hand up and down Bern's chest.

* * * *

Oh my God, Jenna had never orgasmed like that in her life. She felt like her world had split into a million pieces and then come back together again, and that was just with his mouth! God, what was it going to be like when he was actually inside her? She couldn't wait to find out.

For now, she had her sexy bear mate in her bed and his express permission to explore at her will and, oh boy, was she going to take advantage of that. She was curled up into his side and running her hands up and down his furry chest. God, it felt so good. His chest hair was wiry and coarse, she bet it would feel marvelous rubbing against her bare breasts.

She sought out his nipples in the pelt of hair and was thrilled to see them pucker and stand at attention when she twirled a finger across the small nubs. Did a man get the same pleasure as a woman from having his nipples played with? She leaned forward and licked one of the small brown discs and Bern moaned. Hmm, it appeared he liked that. So, Jenna sucked his nipple and nipped it lightly with her teeth. Bern growled. Oh, he really liked that.

Jenna kissed down his chest and followed the happy trail that lead to the waistband of his pants. Just how bold did she dare to be? Bern had performed oral sex on her, could she do the same for him? She'd seen it done on porno videos. He was her mate, she'd give it her best shot.

She popped the button on his pants and the head of his cock popped out. Commando. Why wasn't she surprised? She gingerly slid down his zipper over the large bulge underneath. Damn, that couldn't be comfortable. Tentatively she kissed the bulbous head and a drop of pre-cum leaked from the slit. She swiped it with her tongue, salty and musky, but not bad tasting.

Jenna slipped her hands into the sides of Bern's pants and worked them over his hips, he lifted to help her slide them down. She removed his shoes and socks when she got to his feet, tossing them off the side of the bed, followed by his pants. Then she stared at the naked man before her, laid out on her bed like a smorgasbord and decided she was really hungry.

Starting at his feet she kissed and caressed her way up his body. She wanted to touch and taste every part of him. Bern was so handsome. Solid sculpted muscle, not an ounce of fat on him, covered in that glorious pelt of man fur. God how she loved hairy men.

She rubbed her cheek against his thighs and nuzzled the crease between his thigh and groin. A low groan came from Bern and he spread his legs wider on the bed. Jenna licked the crease, teasing. With one finger, she traced the line on his sac between his balls, then up the thick vein on his cock, before cupping him in her palm.

Her tongue followed her hand and she licked along the vein and then engulfed him in her mouth. "Jenna," he groaned. "Sweet heaven, baby. Your mouth is so hot."

Jenna pulled back and licked the slit teasing the opening of his dick and stealing the pre-cum that was leaking from it. Then she took as much of him as she could into her mouth, establishing an up and down rhythm that had Bern thrusting his hips off the bed and panting within moments. He grabbed her by the hair and pulled her off his dick.

"Stop, mate or we will be finished before we start," he said, pulling her up the bed and kissing her until her toes curled. He flipped her to her back and kissed down her neck, finding that spot behind her ear that made her shiver. His beard tickled and aroused at the same time, she loved the way it felt scraping across her skin.

As he kissed his way to her breasts, one of his hands slid down her body to toy with her mound. She was already slick with cream, pleasuring him had turned her on big time. He slipped a finger inside and sucked a nipple into his mouth at the same time. Her body was receiving so many pleasurable signals it didn't know what to do. She arched and squirmed, crying out for Bern. She needed something, but she really didn't know what at this point in time.

"You're so wet, little one," he said as he added a second finger. He pressed his thumb to her clit and she mewled.

"I need you, Bern. I want you inside me."

He leapt from the bed and extracted a condom from his wallet. He was sheathed and back between her legs before she had drawn a breath. When Jenna felt the huge breadth of his cock at the entrance to her pussy she felt a moment's trepidation.

"Hush, my pet. It will be fine. I'll go slow. Just relax" He kissed her gently and all the nervousness left her body.

Bern pushed forward gently and Jenna felt a burning sensation, a fullness, but it wasn't too bad. He kissed and caressed her, murmuring words she didn't really hear or understand, nonsense words, love words. He was moving very slowly back and forth, pushing forward a little more each time, it was uncomfortable, but not horrible, then he pulled back and slammed forward, and there was a stabbing pain. Jenna cried out.

"I'm sorry, baby. It will stop in a minute. Just let your body adjust." Bern kissed her eyelids, her temple, her cheek her neck, Jenna slowly relaxed and the pain subsided.

"Okay now?" Bern asked.

"Yes." She nodded

Bern began to move. Slowly sliding in and out. The hair on his chest rubbed against her nipples and she was right, it did feel good, damn good. Now that the pain was gone the feeling of Bern moving inside her was good too. Jenna began to pick up the rhythm and move with him. She locked her legs around his hips to draw him closer. This changed the angle of his penetration and his pelvic bone hit her clitoris with every forward thrust. She ground her hips against him, straining for that last spark of sensation needed to come. Bern reached for her breast and pinched her nipple and that was it, she exploded like a star going super nova.

Her pussy clamped down on Bern and milked him to his climax and he came with her, shouting her name in ecstasy as he shot his seed into the latex covering inside her. He collapsed onto his elbows above her and rolled them to their sides.

Jenna lay with her head pillowed on Bern's considerable bicep as her breathing returned to normal. She was a hot sweaty mess, her hair was plastered to her face and she felt like she'd run a marathon. Hell, her legs were shaking. Who knew sex was so…exhausting, she thought as her eyes drifted closed and slumber stole her thoughts.

Jenna woke to find the bed next to her empty and the smell of food enticing her to the kitchen. She rose from the bed gingerly, used the restroom, brushed her teeth, slipped on her robe and sauntered into the kitchen to find her big bear at the stove in nothing but his jeans and bare feet. That was a sight she could certainly get used to.

She stole up behind him and wrapped her arms around his waist.

"Did you have a nice nap, little one?"

"I did," she said with a sheepish grin. "Someone wore me out."

Bern smiled down at her, looking a bit prideful. "Dinner is almost ready. Why don't you pour yourself a glass of wine and rest while I finish cooking?"

"Man, a girl could get used to this kind of pampering," Jenna said, pulling his head down to kiss his lips before doing as he suggested.

Once Jenna was seated at the table she said. "I guess we really should talk about the rest of the stuff, we kind of got distracted from earlier? Huh?"

Bern raised an eyebrow. "I guess so. Though, I must say, I myself am very glad we got distracted."

Jenna could feel the blush color her cheeks. "Me too."

Bern came over to the table and kissed her heartily.

"Okay, where shall we start this time?"

"Well, let's go back to what happened at the store. I understand now why Andy was so differential to you, but what was the big deal about that wolf being in the store? There are wolves all over Honey Corners."

"There are wolves in Honey Corners, yes, but they are wolves not associated with a pack. Lone wolves, or wolves that we have adopted into our clan. The wolf that was in Andy's store was part of the Von Drake pack. They live in the next town over. It is hard to explain…We are friendly rivals, I guess would be the best way to put it. We are not at war, but not exactly friends either. We do not trust each other. Pack/clan members are not allowed to travel into each other's territory without permission and the borders are guarded."

"So, that wolf should not have been here without permission?"

"Correct, but more importantly, he shouldn't have been able to get to where he was without being detected. That's the part that has me upset."

"And the wolf who invited us to dinner, Von Drake. Since the pack is named Von Drake, I'm assuming he's the head wolf?"

"Yes, he is the alpha."

"So, how the hell does he know about me?"

"That is the other question that sticks in my craw. He should not know about you already. I have told the clan…"

"You what?"

"I told the clan."

"When the hell did you do that?"

"The day we met."

"You told the whole town we were mates the day you met me?"

"Yes, of course."

"What do you mean? Yes, of course. Don't you think that was a little presumptuous?"

"No. It was necessary. I had to make sure you were protected."

"What are you talking about?"

"You have been guarded since I found out you were my mate."

Jenna thought her head might just explode. *No wonder I felt like I was being watched! I was being watched! Gah!*

"People have been spying on me?"

"No one has been spying on you. Someone has just been posted outside your domicile to make sure you were safe and unharmed."

"They followed me when I walked to school too, didn't they?"

"Yes."

"That's why I had that creepy feeling I was being watched, I thought I was being paranoid or going crazy! Why didn't you tell me?"

"I hadn't told you I was *Sippe Leiter* yet. How could I explain you might be in danger from being my mate? Plus, I didn't want you to be afraid. I never thought you would even notice my guards, they must be slipping, you should never have known they were there."

"Well, I did know they were there, I even told you about my creepy feeling and you didn't say anything then." Jenna punched him in the shoulder and then shook her hand out. Damn, it was like hitting concrete.

Bern grabbed her hand and kissed her fingers. "I'm sorry you hurt your hand, and I'm sorry I didn't say anything when you mentioned it. I didn't want you to be mad at me," he said with a silly fake pout on his face. Jenna couldn't help but laugh.

"Okay, I forgive you." She kissed him and plopped back onto her chair.

Bern turned back to the stove and pulled the salmon from under the broiler, it smelled delicious. Jenna stood and retrieved plates from the cabinet and silverware from the drawer. Bern served up the salmon along with steamed broccoli and parmesan pasta and they ate in silence for a few minutes.

"This is wonderful," Jenna said.

"Anything would be wonderful with you for company," Bern replied.

Can this really be happening to me? Jenna smiled across the table at her mate.

"So, is this dinner with the Von Drake wolf a big deal?"

"Yes, my second, Martin will be having a fit over it. We do not often associate with the Von Drake wolves and if we do it is in neutral territory, never in their den."

"Are we going to go?"

"I'm afraid we have little choice. To decline would be an insult. It could cause us to go to war."

"Is it dangerous?"

"It could be, but I don't think so. We will be going into Von Drake territory, but we will take a few guards with us. However, Von Drake knows that if he issues an invitation and perpetrates aggression on me or my mate it will mean full out war. I don't think he would be that stupid."

"Okay."

They finished dinner and did the dishes together, brushing hands and rubbing against each other constantly. They moved into the living room, popped a movie in the DVD player and snuggled up on the couch.

Bern sat in the corner of the overstuffed sofa and Jenna sprawled across his lap, she was much more interested in him than she was the *Werewolf of London.* Suddenly a thought popped into her head from her paranormal romance books about mating.

Jenna abruptly sat up. "Bern, when, um I mean if we mate, you bite me right?"

Bern smiled at her slip of the tongue. "Yes, little one."

"Um…this may be a stupid question, but…"

"Go ahead and ask, sweetness, nothing you ask is stupid."

"Will I, um, turn into a werebear?" Jenna bit her lip.

Bern looked down at her and smiled. "Did you read that in one of your romance novels?"

Jenna gave a sheepish shrug, "Yeah, I said it was a silly question."

Bern turned seriously. "You have to understand, little one, what I am about to tell you cannot be shared with anyone. It is a secret closely guarded by the shifter world."

Jenna swallowed tightly. "I promise."

"Yes, you will change."

Jenna gasped.

"But, understand, this only works for mates. It's not like we can go around biting people and changing them into weres. The goddess gave us this gift, because a were's life span is so much longer than a human's. If we couldn't turn our mate then we would be destined to live much of our life alone."

"Wow. That's something I'd never thought of. So, how long will I live?"

"Barring an accident or war, you could live to be six or seven hundred years old."

"Seriously? That's a long damn time. I'll out live all my friends, my family."

"You would have out lived your parents anyway you know. You will make friends among the weres. My sisters will love you, I know. You will have more family than you know what to do with."

Jenna smiled. "It would be nice to have sisters. I always wanted a sister."

"I will be happy to share mine with you." Bern kissed the tip of her nose.

She laid her head against his chest and hugged him close. He bent down and began kissing along her jawline. Soon her robe had fallen open and Bern's hands were roaming freely across her body. Jenna slipped from the couch and switched off the TV.

"Let's go to bed," she said and her big bear followed her into the bedroom. Where he made sweet love to her before she drifted off to sleep in his big hairy arms.

Chapter Five

The buzzing of her alarm clock roused Jenna from a deep sleep, she tried to reach over to hit the snooze button, but something held her trapped in place. She looked down, found a furry arm surrounding her naked torso and grinned. The massive body behind her shifted, pulling closer and growled. Jenna chuckled. "I need to turn off the alarm."

His beard covered face nuzzled behind her ear "Mmm, yes turn off that noise, so I can snuggle with you."

"No, silly. While that would be nice, I have to get up. It's a school day." She patted the hand that covered her stomach in a silent demand for him to release her.

"But, Mom, I don't wanna go to school," he whined. "Call in sick." He squeezed her tight and buried his head in her back. All the while the alarm blared in the background.

Jenna finally managed to reach her arm out and slap the alarm silent. She turned in Bern's arms and cupped his face. "I would like nothing better than to spend the day in bed with you, my honey bear, but a room full of sweet little smiling faces will be waiting for me in…" She looked over her shoulder at the clock. "Oh my goodness, an hour. I've got to get a move on!" Jenna jumped from the bed, and Bern grabbed for her, but his arms snagged empty air.

Jenna rushed into the bathroom and flipped on the shower while she brushed her teeth. "The coffee maker is on a timer, so there's coffee in the kitchen, help yourself," she called as she dropped her toothbrush and stepped into the warm shower. She started when a large body followed her behind the zebra stripped curtain.

"Opp! Bern, what are you doing in here?"

"Taking a shower, what does it look like?"

"With me?" she squeaked.

"Sure," he said planting a kiss on her nose. Saves water. Jenna ducked her head under the shower, she shouldn't be embarrassed after everything they'd done together last night, but somehow showering together seemed more intimate then having sex. It was mundane and every day.

Jenna quickly shampooed and conditioned her hair, and then moved out of the way of the water so Bern could utilize the stream. The confines of her shower had never seemed so small. Jenna squirted a generous dollop of vanilla scented bath gel onto a bath puff and started soaping her body.

When she looked up Bern's eyes were glowing an uncanny amber instead of the normal deep chocolate she had come to love. "Bern," she gasped, "Your eyes…"

He closed his eyes for a moment and when he opened them they were chocolate colored once again. He pulled her close, rubbing her soap covered body against his and kissing the top of her head. "I'm sorry, little one. I didn't mean to startle you. My bear was a bit near the surface, your luscious scent has him rather aroused this morning."

Jenna stepped back and looked up into Bern's face. "Really? We don't have time now, but…can I see your bear soon? Will you show me?"

"Of course, I will be glad to show you my bear. He would love to show off for you. Would you like to come to my house tonight? There are lots of woods around there, so it's safe for me to change."

"Okay. That sounds good. Oh God. I really need to hurry. I'm going to be late."

They both rinsed and jumped from the shower. Bern dressed quickly in his jeans from the night before and kissed Jenna on the cheek. "I will go and get your coffee ready. Do you want anything to eat?"

"Some toast would be great, thanks," Jenna said as she rummaged through her drawers for underwear. The numbers on the clock seemed to be flipping at an alarmingly rapid rate and perspiration was coating her skin. Great. That would make getting dressed so much fun.

Bern left the room and she took a moment to stand under the blades of the ceiling fan and take a deep breath and relax. So much had changed in her life since yesterday, she needed to calm down and find her center. Everything that happened had been good, marvelous in fact. She needed to remember that. Yes, things were happening fast, but that wasn't a bad thing. Up until now her life had been a slow crawl, maybe it was about time things sped up, she laughed.

Cooled off and calmed down she donned a flowing crochet maxi skirt in deep purple, one of her favorites and a cream colored embroidered top. She quickly blew her hair dry and put it up in a messy bun on top of her head, a light application of makeup, her espadrilles and she was ready to go.

Jenna walked into her kitchen and stopped, Bern stood at the sink, a cup of coffee in his hand staring out the window over the sink as she often did in the morning. He was shirtless and shoeless and oh so handsome. He must have heard her enter, because he turned and flashed her a panty dropping smile, white teeth flashing from his neatly trimmed beard.

"Your coffee and toast are on the table." He crossed to give her a kiss. "Let me get my shirt and shoes and I'll walk you to school.

When they stepped onto the front porch a large blond man emerged from the shadows a few hundred feet from the property line. He opened the gate for us to exit and nodded to Bern and then to me. "Good morning, *Sippe*."

"Morning, Hans. All is well?"

"Yes, *Sippe*."

"Very good. You're dismissed. I'll walk Miss Jenna to school today."

"*Danke*, *Sippe*," Hans said with a small salute as he strode away.

"I knew the town had an old German look to it, but I didn't realize that people still spoke the language."

"The clan is originally from Germany. My family is from Stuttgart. We have only been in America one generation, my parents came from Germany. Many have been here longer, but still, for clan business, things are often done in the old language."

"Wow, you learn something new every day. Lately I feel like my brain is on overload." Jenna paused for a moment. "I talked to my best friend, Alice the other day, I told her about you."

Bern leaned his head onto her shoulder, "You did, did you? And what did you say?"

Jenna could feel heat rush to her cheeks. "That is privileged information. Don't you know the girl code?"

"Girl code?"

"Yes. Anything that best friends say to each other is off limits to boyfriends."

Bern smiled smugly, and waggled his eyebrows, "So, I'm your boyfriend now, am I?"

Jenna slugged him on the arm. "Well, I certainly wouldn't have slept with you if I didn't consider you my boyfriend," she hissed, shaking her throbbing hand. Damn his arm was hard.

"I want to invite Alice to come down and meet you. Is that okay?"

"Of course. I'd love to meet your friend."

Jenna hugged Bern's arm, it felt so nice walking and talking with him. Maybe there really was something to this mate bond thing, because they just 'clicked.' Bern was so easy to talk to, he put her at ease, made her feel comfortable about herself. Safe. Secure…loved.

Too soon the brick façade of the school appeared. Bern escorted her right to the door and left her with a gentle kiss on the lips.

* * * *

Bern entered his office and as expected found Martin already there and trying to pace a hole in the hardwood floor. His lieutenant, Guiles was seated on the sofa, drinking a cup of coffee and eating a honey bun.

"I told him to sit down and relax," Guiles said, "But, you know Martin. The world is coming to an end and if he just keeps pacing it will stall the inevitable."

Bern laughed and reached for the pot of coffee on his desk, he poured a cup and added plenty of sugar and cream, then he sat down behind the desk and took a long sip before directing his attention to Martin.

"*Zweite, sitzen sie!* Second, sit. You are making me nervous!"

Martin sat on the edge of the arm chair facing Bern's desk. "What are we going to do about Von Drake?"

"We aren't going to do anything. Jenna and I will go to dinner, with a few guards of course as a precaution, and hopefully have a lovely time."

"Are you insane? What if it's a trap?"

Bern raised one eyebrow at Martin, and a low growl issued from his throat. The look in his eye guaranteed to quell the attitude coming from his subordinate.

"Um…I'm sorry, *Sippe*. I did not mean to question your judgment."

"Von Drake is not a fool. If he wanted to set a trap for Jenna or me, he would not send out an invitation. Why not just paint a big red target on his own back? Everyone in our clan would know he was the culprit and none would stop until he was destroyed." Bern rose and walked to Martin's side, slamming his fingers against Martin's temples. "Think man, think. He would have to be the insane one to try something like that."

Martin looked down and to the left, baring his neck to his alpha. "You are right, sir."

Bern leaned forward and hugged his second, placing his forehead to the other man's for a moment. "I appreciate your concern, my friend. You are a good second, but you must learn to curb your hot head and think things through. You are young yet. Time will teach you well."

Bern turned to Guiles, "Did you determine how the young wolf got through our defenses?"

"No, that is the part that has me stumped. It's almost like he had a cloaking spell. None of our trackers could find any hint of his scent, either from his coming or his leaving."

"I smelled his scent clearly enough in Andy's store," Bern interjected.

"I know, that's what makes it so odd."

"We searched the area, but couldn't find any tracks or scent." Guiles studied the pattern in the throw rug on the floor. "I'm sorry, sir. I don't know what else to do."

"Step up patrols in the area along the western border. Add some wolves to those patrolling that sector, maybe they'll smell something we're missing."

"Yes, sir."

Bern went back behind his desk and poured another cup of coffee. "Anything else I need to know about?"

Martin cleared his throat. "Janice Hilliard's son, Boyd saw a man with an infrared scope and a tranq gun sneaking around the edge of town after dark last night. He followed him back to a camp about ten miles outside town. Boyd told his momma, and she told her friends and you know how that goes. Now the whole town is rumbling about, HUNTS Humans United Negation Team for Shifters."

"Crap, that's all we need."

"It's just rumors at this point, but I think we should check it out."

"Definitely, better safe than sorry, but I don't want any trouble. Send a recon team in first. Find out if these yahoos are even in the hate group to start with before we do anything. If they are, then we'll have to decide what to do. For the moment, do not approach them. Investigate, only. Understand?"

Both men stood. "Yes, sir," they answered together.

"We done for now?"

They nodded, "Dismissed." Bern flipped on his computer and Guiles and Martin left the room.

Bern tried to concentrate on the invoices for his lumber company, but he couldn't get the thought of the possible threat to his clan out of his mind. Were the campers in the woods really from the HUNTS group or was his clan merely being paranoid?

Shifters had never been a threat to the human race. While by nature shifters were violent, violence against humans had never been tolerated. It was a death sentence to a shifter to attack a human. Before they had come out, it was necessary to keep their secret, now it was necessary to keep the peace that balanced on the head of a pin.

Shifters were stronger and faster than humans, they healed faster and lived longer, but in one area they were seriously lacking. Numbers. Shifters were outnumbered by humans by millions to one. If the human population decided they truly were a threat they would end up in cages or worse.

Shifters would be forced to go back into hiding, living in the wild, or in a cage. Not much of a choice. While Bern loved his bear, he loved his human half too. He had no desire to live a feral life. He liked living in a house, shopping in stores and eating cooked food. Hey, he was a civilized bear.

If however, the men in the woods turned out to be from HUNTS there was no reason they couldn't just 'disappear.' His bear murmured his approval.

Bern turned his attention back to his computer and the invoices. The day passed quickly and before he knew it the alarm on his wristwatch was dinging, three o'clock. Time to go and pick up his pretty Jenna.

* * * *

John Reed drove deep into the Smokey Mountains. The location of the research facility was hidden from everyone, it couldn't even be found on satellite as it was buried deep underneath the mountain. He wanted to check on the status of the wolf cubs they had acquired, aka kidnapped, one last week and one a month ago.

He pulled up to what looked like a solid rock wall and stopped his truck. Exiting he found the hidden panel and entered the code that opened the wall. The shifters knew of the existence of HUNTS, but what they didn't know, what most of the members of HUNTS didn't even know, was that a secret branch of the government was funding the organization. They had their own agenda, and John was part of that plan. A former Special Forces operative, he knew the secrets others only dreamed about, or found in their worst nightmares, depending on your perspective.

A massive compound thrived inside the mountain. John parked just outside the elevators to the lower levels. He swiped his security pass and descended to the seventh level, Doctor Montrose's laboratory.

The elevator doors swung open to reveal a pristine laboratory, complicated machines and gadgets covered every surface, gleaming stainless steel tables, and glass fronted cabinets. White coated technicians scurried about, doing who knows what, but what drew John's attention were the glass cages along the wall containing the specimens he and his brethren had collected.

Six of the cages were now full, they needed a total of ten to complete the testing. Doctor Montrose looked up from her microscope and spotted him. "John, how good to see you."

"Hello, Doc. How are things going?"

"Wonderful, the testing is going well. I think we are really on to something this time," she replied.

"No problems with the new specimens?" he asked.

"Oh, the usual. We are keeping them sedated at the moment. How are you coming on the acquisition of the bears?" she asked.

"We should have them within the next week," he answered.

"Good, good. That will only leave us in need of the lions. Do you have a lead on where we can acquire them?"

"Yes, I have found a Pride in Arizona. We will be heading there when we leave West Virginia," John said.

"That's wonderful."

"So, you've made progress on the serum?"

"You know I'm not at liberty to discuss the results of the tests in progress with you, John," Doctor Montrose said with a note of censure.

"And you know what I want to know, Elizabeth! Have there been any more *accidents*?"

Doctor Montrose flushed bright red. Whether in anger or embarrassment it was impossible to tell. "No, John. No more accidents."

John nodded. "I'll be going then. I'll be back in a few days with the bears."

He drove back to his camp deep in thought about what was to come.

Five men sat around a camp fire ten miles west of Honey Corners. They didn't bother to hide their location, if anyone came by they would claim to be fisherman on a camping trip.

John, addressed the men, "What did you find out last night, Scott?"

"Nothing we didn't expect. We are definitely not going to be able to get ahold of a kid outside at night. I swear they roll up the sidewalks in this town at dark. Mr. and Mrs. Bear sit on their front porch drinking tea and rocking in their chairs, while Johnny Bearcat is down at the lake spooning with his girl and the three little bears are tucked up in their den watching TV. It's like a rerun of fucking Mayberry RFD. It isn't fair that these *abominations* are out here living the American dream while I had to watch my beautiful wife die of ovarian cancer at thirty-five! Why don't they get sick? Why do they live so long? It just isn't fair!"

John patted him on the back. "I know friend. I know."

Scott looked up at him with tear filled eyes. "But I don't want to turn into one of those monsters. I don't want to be an animal or, God forbid, one of those mutant creatures that the first experiments created."

"Yeah or die," Kyle muttered.

"That's not going to happen," John said. "It has to be an antibody in the blood, not something in the DNA sequencing, we just have to isolate it. I know the team of scientists we have put together now can do it. Soon we will eradicate cancer from the world."

"And those degenerate shifters too," Scott murmured.

"In time," John agreed. "We have to make sure we have all the answers, before we eliminate the source of the antibodies."

"Okay, so what's the plan?" Kyle asked.

"We'll stick with what we did in the wolf den. Gas the house while the bears are sleeping, and be done before they wake up."

"Do you have enough of that scent blocker to cover our tracks?" Scott asked.

"I've got plenty," John replied. "Let's do a recon mission into town tomorrow and then we can plan the abduction. Maybe we can even pick out a target." The man was practically rubbing his hands together in anticipation.

He had been planning this mission for two long years and nothing was going to stand in his way. He was going to capture a shifter child and they were going to find out the secret to these shifters long lives and health if it was the last thing he did on this earth.

Chapter Six

As the students filed out of the classroom at the end of the day, Sarah came up to Jenna's desk. Her brown hair was fashioned into long braids on either side of her round little face, freckles sprinkled across her pert nose. She looked down at her Maryjanes and rocked from heel to toe.

Jenna squatted down so they were face to face. "What's up, Miss Sarah?"

"My mommy said you're gonna be my new aunt, Miss Raynes. That you're Unca Bern's mate, is that true?"

Jenna laughed a little self-consciously. "Um, yes. Your uncle and I are mates. Is that okay with you?"

Sarah beamed up at her. "That's super cool! I love Unca Bern, he's my favrotist. All my other uncas are only my aunt's husbands, ya know," she whispered. "Unca Bern is my *real* unca."

Jenna wasn't quite sure what to say to this revelation, she certainly didn't want to get into family politics already, or step on any toes. Thank goodness Bern walked in the door at just that moment.

"Well, lookie here, my two favorite girls, in one place," he said, walking over and kissing Jenna sweetly and then hoisting Sarah high in the air and twirling her in a circle. She threw her arms around his neck and peppered kisses all over his face.

"I loves you, Unca Bern."

"I love you too, sweet Sarah. Where's your momma?"

"I don't know, she must be late. You know she's *always* late," the little girl replied.

"That she is," Bern said, turning to Jenna. "Julia was even born late. I swear that woman is never on time for anything."

Julia rushed into the room, a toddler on her hip, a diaper bag and a purse hanging off her shoulder, her hair falling out of a messy bun on the top of her head and looking like she'd had a day from hell. "Oh my God, Miss Raynes, I'm so sorry! Jimmy is sick and I was at the pharmacy picking up his medicine. The line was terrible. I hope I didn't hold you up."

"Not at all. Sarah and I were just chatting until Bern got here, and please call me Jenna."

The baby in her arms started to fuss and Bern reached out and plucked the boy from her hip. "What's the matter little man? You not feeling well?" Bern arched a brow at his sister.

"He's teething."

"Oh, that explains it. Little bears have some big teeth to come in at his age. I know you've met before, but Jenna, this is my sister, Julia."

"I'm so happy Bern has finally met his mate, and I couldn't be happier to welcome you to the family. We'll have to all get together soon and have a big family dinner."

Bern bounced Jimmy on his hip and the baby seemed perfectly happy now. Seeing him with Sarah and now Jimmy made her think he'd be a wonderful father. Whoa, slow down girl, let's not put the cart before the horse, but she couldn't help smiling at the thought of Bern holding a tiny baby in his big bear paws.

"That sounds great. Call me later in the week and we can set up a date."

"Wonderful. Bern would you mind helping me get these two out to the car?"

Bern looked at Jenna, she nodded. "Sure, no problem." He linked his free hand with hers and they strolled out to the parking lot.

Bern strapped Jimmy into his car seat while Julia loaded Sarah into hers. He kissed his sister on the cheek and patted the top of the SUV before she drove away.

"Are you ready to go?"

"Sure," she said.

"Well, I'm not." He pulled her into the shadow of a tall oak tree and crushed her body to his. Capturing her head in his hands he held her in place as his mouth took possession of hers in a most carnal way. His tongue swept in, stealing her breath, he tasted of brown sugar and maple. She melted into him, sliding her arms around his thick neck to twine in the long hair at his nape.

When he finally came up for air, she was panting for breath and could barely stand on legs that felt like over-cooked spaghetti. "I've been waiting to do that all day, little one. God, how I've missed you," Bern growled.

"Wow, a girl could get used to a hello like that, big guy."

"Mmm, you better," he said, with another quick peck to her lips, "because I plan to kiss you like that every day for the rest of our lives."

Now that was a promise Jenna certainly hoped he kept. Bern stepped back and took her hand. They started walking toward the outskirts of town. She wondered if he owned a car, he seemed to walk everywhere, just like she did.

They walked for quite a while in silence, but it was a companionable silence. The fall day was beautiful, cool but not cold. Colored leaves covered the trees and drifted to the ground, crunching under their feet occasionally as they walked along.

The trail began a steady uphill grade, until finally they reached the top of a high hill. There sat what Jenna could only describe as a mansion. A sprawling Tudor mansion, with massive oak front doors, surrounded by beautiful forest. It was perhaps the most beautiful house she had ever seen.

She stopped dead in her tracks and her hands came up to cover her mouth. "Oh my God."

Bern turned to her, worry evident on his face. "What's the matter?"

"It's beautiful," she said in an awed voice. "You really live here? It's a freakin' mansion."

Bern shook his head. "It's not a mansion. It's just a house. A big house, yes, but just a house." He tugged her hand to get her moving again. "Come inside and let me show it to you."

Jenna hesitated, pulling against his hand. "I don't know. Maybe I should just stay here and look from outside. I don't want to break anything."

Bern cocked a brow at her. "Are you kidding me? I am a ten foot grizzly bear, if I haven't broken it already, you certainly aren't going to break it."

Jenna laughed. Bern knew how to break the tension. He was right, she was being silly. She followed him into the house and tried her best to keep her exclamations of awe to herself, but *damn*, this place was something else.

From the stained glass windows in the foyer, to the kitchen that looked like something out of Better Homes and Gardens magazine, Jenna was completely out of her element. Her parents weren't poor by any stretch of the imagination, they were middle class, but this...this was, well she wasn't quite sure what this was, but it was definitely high class and then some.

Bern seemed to sense her nervousness and he led her into a cozy den. *Ha ha, den for a bear, I think I'm getting slaphappy.*

"How about a glass of wine? I've got a nice white zinfandel in the fridge."

"That sounds good," Jenna said.

Bern crossed to the bar on the side of the room and reached into the small refrigerator, he pulled out a bottle of white zinfandel and using a corkscrew from on top of the bar uncorked the wine. He poured two glasses and crossed to Jenna with the glasses in hand.

He sat beside her on the small couch and placed the glass in her hand, then he clinked their glasses together. "To a life time of nights together," he said as he brought the glass to his lips.

Jenna hid her smile behind her glass as she took a sip. How did she get so lucky? She was really waiting for the guy from *Candid Camera* or *Punked* to pop out and tell her this was all a big joke, because the too big, too fat, awkward girl just didn't get the hunky guy, who by the way just happened to be the freaking alpha of a bear clan. In what universe did that happen? Maybe in the *Twilight Zone,* geeze, she really needed to stop watching late night television.

"I'm gonna go scrounge us up some snacks," Bern said, he flipped the stereo on as he left the room and his customary country music flowed from the speakers hidden somewhere in the room. Jenna snuggled down into the couch and let her mind drift with the music as she sipped her wine. She was going to get to see Bern shift tonight. She was a little nervous, but a lot excited.

She'd never seen a shifted bear up close. Enough was enough, as soon as he got back she was going to ask him to shift, the anticipation was killing her. She was never going to be able to relax until after he shifted.

Bern came back into the room carrying a tray of cheese and crackers. Her stomach growled. Okay, maybe she would eat something before she asked him to shift, and make sure he did too, she certainly didn't want a hungry bear on her hands. Jenna stifled a giggle and Bern gave her a curious look. Jenna chose to pretend she didn't notice and dove into the cheese and crackers he had placed on the coffee table.

She crunched a few crackers and took a few sips of wine. Bern lounged at the opposite end of the sofa doing the same, but watching her intently. Finally she had enough. "What? Do I have cracker crumbs on my mouth or something?"

"No, but you are hiding something. What's going on in that brain of yours, little one?"

"Is this more of that mate bond thing? Because if it is, I don't think I like it."

"No, it's not the mate bond. I'm just getting to know you, and I can see the little hamster wheel turning in your head."

"Hey, I resemble that remark!"

Bern moved so that his knee was touching hers on the sofa and kissed her temple. "I'm sorry, little one. I was only teasing. You have a big, beautiful, brain." He punctuated each word with a kiss. "I only meant I can tell something is bothering you. He cupped her face in his hands and stared down into her eyes, "Tell me, what's wrong?"

Jenna felt like a stupid fool. "Nothing is wrong, per se. I'm just nervous about seeing you shift."

"I don't have to shift today."

"No," she practically shouted. "I'm sorry. I want you to shift. I really want to see your bear. I'm just a little scared. I know it's stupid. I know it's still you when you shift…"

"Yes, it is, but I am different too. There are a few things I want to tell you before I shift. First and most important. Don't run from me. While I still remain in control of my human thought when I shift, I also have…baser animal instincts. My bear, he wants you very much. If you run, he will chase you. He would never hurt you, but he will give chase, and I don't want him to scare you."

"Okay." Jenna nodded.

"Second, obviously I won't be able to talk to you when I shift. After we are mated and you change we will be able to communicate telepathically when we are shifted."

Jenna gasped. "I didn't know you could do that."

"No, most humans don't."

"Wow, that's really cool."

"Yes, it is a wonderful gift. Anyway, I won't be able to talk to you now, and I won't be able to shift back for a few minutes. It takes a lot of energy to shift. So just sit quietly with me and wait. Okay?"

"Yes."

"Are you ready?"

"Yes."

Bern stood and pushed the coffee table to the side of the room, then he started to strip out of his clothes.

"What are you doing?"

"Taking my clothes off."

Jenna could feel the blush coloring her cheeks. "What the hell for?"

"Because if I shift with them on I will either shred them or strangle on them."

Duh, Jenna you are really not thinking tonight. "I never thought of that. I guess I thought maybe they just disappeared and reappeared when you shifted back."

"Damn, that would be a nice trick. It would have saved me from a lot of embarrassing situations in the past too, I can tell you, but no, doesn't happen."

Jenna cleared her throat and looked at the floor. "You're not going to see me change if you're looking at the rug," Bern teased. "It's not like you haven't seen me naked before, you know."

"That was different," Jenna grumbled.

Bern laughed. "Well it's your choice, but don't complain to me if you miss the show."

Jenna looked up and glared at him. Bern looked smug, the bastard, and in the next moment her big bear of a man was…well a big bear. There was no cracking of bones or noise, like she expected, no flash of white light, in fact it was so fast, if she'd have blinked she'd have missed it. One minute he was a man, the next he was a bear. Magic.

He stood for a moment on his hind legs, startling her with his size. Bern stood about ten feet tall, covered in brown fur tipped with a light gold at the ends. His chocolate brown eyes were now that eerie amber color, and claws over two inches long extended from the end of his paws.

He dropped to all fours on the floor and then lay down on his belly, resting his head on his paws and Jenna swore he was trying to give her an innocent look. He nodded his head and made a cuffing noise deep in his throat.

Jenna scooched to the edge of the couch and waggled her fingers at Bern. "Hi."

The big goof tipped his head to the side and let his tongue hang out. Oh boy that was one long tongue. Jenna got down onto the floor and crawled toward Bern. He chuffed his encouragement and she laughed. When she reached his head she asked. "Is it okay if I pet you? I forgot to ask before you shifted."

The big bear awkwardly nodded its head and Jenna gently stroked the fur between his eyes. He crept closer until his head was resting in her lap and she was scratching behind his ears. A sound almost like a purr resonated from the bear's chest. "Oh you like that, do you?"

Jenna was astonished at the feel of the bear's fur. The outside was coarse and stiff, almost wiry, but underneath it was soft as down. She bent her face down to press it into the scruff of his neck and all at once her lap was no longer full of furry bear, but fully aroused naked man flesh.

In a flash she was on her back with Bern's naked body covering hers. His arousal pressed against her thigh as his lips captured hers in a kiss she might consider giving up double chocolate fudge ice cream for.

Bern kissed her eyelids, her cheeks, her nose, down her neck, then he pulled back and looked deep into her eyes. "We should not have done this... I didn't think." He ground his erection against her and peppered her face with kisses, in a frenzy of motion.

Jenna placed her hands on either side of his face halting his movements. His lower body continued to undulate. "What's the matter, Bern? What's wrong?"

"My bear...he wants you now. Wants to mate. Wants to mark you. Make you ours for always. I don't know if I can hold him back. You should leave."

Jenna released her hold on his head, and he buried his face in her neck. He held her tight, but so carefully, she felt protected, safe, loved. No, she wasn't going to leave. Despite whatever reservations she'd had about the mate bond, she was already in love with Bern. Maybe the goddess did know something after all. She was sure they were meant to be together and she was ready to take the next step.

She stroked the back of the shaggy hair she adored. "It's okay, baby. I'm not going anywhere, but upstairs, with you." Bern pulled back and looked down at her. "Take me to bed, and make me your mate," she said as tears filled her eyes.

Her big naked bear stood with her in his arms and never paused. He took the stairs two at a time until he reached his bedroom on the second floor. Jenna didn't have time to do more than catch a glimpse of his large bedroom before she dropped into the center of a very large soft bed. She didn't bounce as the pillow top and the thick gray comforter absorbed her weight. Bern came down beside her and began stripping off her clothes before she had time to blink.

"I'm sorry, little one. I'm not going to be able to go slow, but I promise I'll make sure you're ready for me," Bern growled as the last of her clothing went sailing over his shoulder.

Frankly his impatience and excitement must be contagious, because Jenna was hot as hell. His cave man, or should she say bear, act had her creaming like Magic Mike was doing a private strip tease all for her.

Bern pressed her knees apart and took a long swipe of her pussy from bottom to top. She shuddered and arched off the bed, keening his name. His tongue circled her clit and he inserted a finger into her channel, pushing deep until he found her sweet spot. One finger became two and he lapped and sucked her clit as he massaged that magic spot inside her until she came screaming his name.

He continued to pump his fingers in and out, slowing his rhythm and gently licking around her clit until she was a quivering mass of Jell-O. His fingers slipped from her mound and he kissed up her rounded belly, stopping to play for a moment with her belly button. His hands came up to grasp her breasts, kneading and plucking at her taut nipples. It felt like there was a string connecting her nipples to her pussy and every time he strummed it both organs vibrated.

Bern played her like a virtuoso. Her body his instrument. He kissed and caressed, tweaked and plucked, until she was trembling on the brink of orgasm without him even penetrating her. He finally reached her mouth and kissed her long and deep, mimicking the act her body longed to complete.

Bern reached to the bedside table for a condom and she whispered in his ear. "I'm on the pill."

He pulled back to look down at her. "I have never taken a woman bare." A shudder wracked his body.

"I think you like the idea."

He buried his mouth in the crease of her neck and shoulder and his cock in her hot sheath at the same time. Jenna arched off the bed and shouted his name in ecstasy. Nothing had ever felt so good.

"Jenna, my Jenna," Bern murmured over and over as he thrust in and out. His arms wrapped around her shoulders holding her in place for his thrusts. Faster and faster, hard and strong, he thrust into her in a driving rhythm in time to the chanting of her name.

He reached between them and thumbed her clit, the last little bit of stimulation she needed to throw her over the edge, and as she threw back her head in climax, Bern struck, biting the flesh between her neck and shoulder and growling out his climax.

There was a brief flash of pain and then Jenna was thrown into a second orgasm, like nothing she had ever felt before in her life. If a normal orgasm was fireworks, this was a star going super nova. The universe exploded, her body split into a million pieces and reformed. Every muscle in her body convulsed, she arched off the bed, hell for a moment she wasn't sure she didn't levitate, and then everything went black.

When she opened her eyes Bern was beside her and there was something cold on her head. She reached up pulled off a cool washcloth. "What happened?"

Bern looked at her with a cocky grin. "You fainted."

She tried to sit up and he pushed her back on the bed. "Seriously?"

"Seriously."

"Oh, crap. You're really gonna have a swelled head now aren't you?"

Bern only smiled and tucked her into his side. Jenna tossed the washcloth over the side of the bed and snuggled up with her bear.

Things could be worse, so she was stuck with a cocky bear. She had an orgasm so hot she passed out. Wait until she told Alice!

Chapter Seven

Jenna dozed a bit snuggled deep in the arms of her big bear, drifting in that wonderful state between real sleep and wakefulness. She was as content as a girl could possibly be, sated beyond belief, happy, relaxed and secure. A loud rumbling from the direction of Bern's stomach broke the serene quiet.

Jenna lifted her head from his shoulder and smiled down at him. "Another country heard from. Is somebody hungry?"

"I could eat a moose," he teased, rolling her over and tickling her neck with his beard. "Let's grab a quick shower and go out for pizza."

"Mmm, pizza, my favorite. You're on, mister."

Jenna made to crawl over Bern to exit the bed, but he snagged her on the way. Playfully biting her butt and then giving it a smack. She yelped and ran toward the bathroom, attempting to shut the door before he could follow.

Bern gave chase and pinned her up against the wall. "What did I tell you about running from me, little one? My bear likes it when its prey runs."

"Oh yeah? And what does your bear do when it catches its prey?" Jenna asked with a saucy wink.

"Why it eats it, my dear," he said with a menacing leer as he backed her into the shower stall. Good God, the shower was as big as her whole bathroom and had six shower heads, Bern hit a control on the wall and they all sprang to life. There was a built in bench along one wall of the shower, and he continued backing her up until her legs hit the edge of the bench.

Steam began to fill the room, and Bern reached down, hooking his hands below her buttocks and lifting her onto the bench. It was the perfect height to put them face to face and he began to kiss her as the gentle cascade of the water wet her hair and slid down her over-sensitive body.

He followed a water droplet down her neck, sipping the moisture from her skin. Jenna leaned back against the wall, the cold tile making her shiver and her already erect nipples peak further. Bern turned his attention to the straining nubs. Licking and sucking, swirling his tongue around the tips and then biting just to the point of pain. Jenna closed her eyes and arched her back, thrusting her chest toward her lover in offering.

Bern brought his hands up to cup her breasts as his mouth continued its downward journey, kissing along her ribcage, the indentation of her waist, dipping into her bellybutton to lap at the water that had pooled in the depression. Her blonde curls were moist from both the shower and her arousal.

Bern continued to massage her breasts while he nuzzled her mound, his nose and lips teasing the small center of her desire. His tongue slipped out and flicked her clit at the same time his fingers pinched her nipples and a cry left her lips.

One hand slid down her body and spread her nether lips, opening them for his exploration. He teased and tormented, licking and sucking her labia and then fucking her with his tongue. All the while his other hand roamed her upper body, massaging and caressing, making her crazy with desire.

He replaced his tongue with his fingers, and moved his mouth back to her clit, circling the outside. Pumping his fingers in and out, she was riding his hand now, right on the edge of coming. "Come for me, little one," he growled, as he bit down on her clit, and she exploded. Clutching his head to her creaming cunt and riding his face to her climax as she screamed his name.

Before she had completely come down from her orgasm Bern was over her, thrusting inside. My, this bench was a convenient accessory. How many times had he used it before? No, she wasn't going to think about things like that. It didn't matter, he was hers now. Forever. That was all that mattered.

She threw her arms around his neck and stroked her hand up and down his broad back. She could feel every muscle contract as he thrust inside her. God her man was sexy. Her hands cupped his ass and what an ass it was, hard and sculpted, like a Greek god. She pulled him impossibly closer, tightening her internal muscles and milking the thick cock inside her.

She ground her hips against him on each upward thrust, matching his pace. Her clit rubbed against his pelvic bone with each movement. Her nails dug into his ass, and her bear seemed to like that as a growl escaped his lips. He leaned forward and his mouth latched onto the place he had bitten her.

They came together, his hot seed filling her pulsing channel as she panted his name, and he sucked a love bite on top of his mating bite on her shoulder.

Bern kissed her lovingly and gently pulled out. "I'm sorry, I shouldn't have done that. Are you sore?"

Jenna was mildly tender, but she wouldn't change anything for the world. "I'm fine," she said, punctuating the statement with a kiss to his lips. She dropped from the bench and reached for the soap and washcloth. She generously lathered the washcloth and began washing her big bear.

He took the soap and washcloth from her and returned the favor. Then reached for the shampoo. "Turn around and let me wash your hair."

Jenna turned and he shampooed her hair, being a man he didn't have any conditioner in the shower and she didn't relish the thought of trying to get a comb through her mass of curls when they got out. Oh, well, she'd have to bring some of her hair care products over. Now wasn't that a thought? She was moving in already.

Bern quickly washed his own hair while she rinsed off and shut off the water. He opened the glass shower door and pulled a heated towel off the rack to pat her dry. Heated towel racks, wow a girl could really get used to this. Jenna now had the chance to finally take a look at the bathroom. It was decadent.

Aside from the huge shower stall they were currently occupying, there was also a black marble Jacuzzi tub big enough for two in the opposite corner. A granite double sink with gold faucets and a black commode. The floor and walls were white marble, giving the room a modern, but fabulous look. Once again it could grace the cover of a magazine.

Jenna wandered back into the bedroom, taking her time to check out the décor, now that urgent matters had been taken care of. Bern's bedroom was the size of her living room. Thick deep, blue carpeting covered the floor. A fireplace took up one whole wall of the room. Set up in front of the fireplace was small sitting area, a loveseat, a big reclining chair, a lamp and end table. A book lay open on the end table and Jenna sauntered over to see what Bern was reading, Dan Brown, interesting.

Bookshelves lined the left of the fireplace and they were overflowing, Jenna smiled. Another thing they had in common, a love of reading. She wandered over to see what books he liked. There was an eclectic mix, everything from dystopian and sci-fi, to murder mysteries and oh my goodness, she saw a few paranormal and erotic romance novels, who would have guessed. Strong arms wrapped around her from behind. "What ya doing?"

"Checking out your books."

"See anything you like?"

"Yeah, actually. I see a few authors I like to read there. I'm a reader too. Glad we have that in common."

"See I told you, the goddess knows."

"Yes, you did." Jenna laughed.

Bern dropped the towel he had been drying with on the chair and Jenna swatted his butt. "Hey," he exclaimed over his shoulder as he walked to the closet and grabbed some jeans, pulling them on commando as usual.

Jenna began to redress in her clothes from the day, while Bern pulled on a polo. As she sat on the bed and slipped on her shoes she asked. "So, I won't change until the full moon right?"

"That's right."

"Will I feel any different between now and then? Because I feel a little weird right now. Like…I can smell you."

Bern laughed. "Yes, that is normal. Your senses will be enhanced a bit, not as much as after the change, but more than you're used to. What do I smell like?" he asked, coming up and taking her in his arms.

Jenna snuggled close. "Yummy," she said.

Bern kissed her nose. "I like yummy," he said.

"So do I." Jenna stood on tiptoe and kissed him tenderly on the mouth.

Bern's stomach growled. "Hold that thought. We need to eat."

"Well, one of us surely does." Jenna laughed.

Bern kept one arm around her shoulders and led her though the house, but not to the front door as they had come in. "I thought we'd drive tonight." They exited into a huge garage. Well the question of whether or not Bern had a car had certainly been answered. There were five cars and three motorcycles in the garage. Jenna was no car expert, in fact she wouldn't know a Maserati from a Mustang, but knew expensive, and there were definitely some expensive cars in this garage.

Everything from a top of the line SUV to a low slung two-seater sports car, wow. Wonder what he was going to pick for their outing tonight? He walked up to the little sports car and opened the passenger door. Jenna slipped into the leather interior and sighed as Bern walked around to the driver's side. It still had that new car smell and the dash gleamed with gadgets and dials.

Bern pressed a button and the garage door behind them opened, he pushed another button on the dash and the car started, no key, man she was way out of her league. "Off we go."

Bern hit the button to close the garage door after they pulled out and they headed downtown to the pizza parlor. There was only one in town, but it was really good, family owned and operated. Of course, Bern knew the owners and they were treated like royalty when they walked in.

"*Sippe Leiter*, how good to see you tonight," Maria said.

"Good to see you too, Maria, and how are Gina and Mario?"

"They are good, sir. Thank you so much for asking. I have a table right over here for you and the lovely lady," Maria said leading them to a table away from most of the others in the restaurant.

As they sat Bern turned to Jenna. "Have you met Jenna yet, Maria?"

"No, *Sippe*."

"Jenna Raynes, my mate. This is Maria Forticola, owner of Roma's Pizza."

Maria looked shocked for a moment, she was one of the clan members who hadn't made it to the impromptu meeting the other night. Then she bowed. "So pleased to meet you, Miss Jenna, *Sippe*, I am so happy for you." She leaned forward and kissed both his cheeks.

"Thank you, Maria. I am a very lucky man."

"Wine! I must bring you some wine to celebrate. I wish I had some champagne, but wine will do. I be right back." Maria scurried away.

Jenna laughed and Bern reached across the table to grasp her hands. "She is so sweet."

"Yes, she is," Bern replied.

"I can't believe she kissed your cheeks like that. Just like an Italian grandma!"

"That's what she is, not mine of course, but of the clan. Maria is over five hundred years old and thinks of herself as grandma to everyone in the clan. She is a good sow."

"Bern! That's not nice."

Bern looked shocked. "What do mean that's not nice?"

"To call her a sow!"

Bern laughed a rich full sound that had everyone in the restaurant turning to look at them. Jenna wanted to crawl under her seat and hide. "A sow is a female bear, Jenna. It is not an insult."

"Oh," Jenna said felling sheepish. "My bad. I knew that. Just testing you."

Bern laughed again.

Maria returned with a bottle of red wine, two glasses and their menus. As she poured the wine Bern said. "I don't think we need menus, unless you want to look Jenna?"

"No, if you know what you want that's fine."

"We'll take two deep dish pies with everything," Bern said.

Maria nodded and slipped away.

"Two?" Jenna asked.

"I'm hungry," Bern replied.

"I guess." Jenna laughed.

Bern rubbed his thumb over the skin on her hands and Jenna heard a voice in her head say "mine" she jumped.

"What is it?" Bern asked.

"Um, you're gonna think I'm crazy, but I just heard a voice in my head."

"You did?"

"Yeah."

"What did it say?"

"Mine."

"Hmm, that's your bear. You're a very advanced girl. It's unusual to have your bear talking to you already. Maybe you have a shifter in your family tree somewhere and you have latent shifter genes so the conversion is happening faster than normal."

"You mean my bear is really like a different person inside me? I thought it was just a part of me. I know you talked about your bear wanting me and stuff, but I didn't get that it was a different person than you."

"It's hard to explain, we are the same person, but different too. We share everything, have the same thoughts and dreams, but he can talk to me, help me, share his strength with me."

"Wow, that's gonna take some getting used to."

"It will be an adjustment, but you will learn to love it. It is very comforting to have your bear with you. I couldn't imagine not having mine with me."

"I guess," Jenna mumbled, not at all sure she was ready for this change in her life. As soon as she was alone she was calling Alice, she needed some best friend advice and reassurance.

Maria came back to the table with the two steaming pizzas and all thoughts of impending changes left Jenna's mind. Garlic and tomato sauce, onion, bell pepper, spicy sausage and pepperoni took center stage.

Maria placed the pies in the center of the table and set small plates in front of Jenna and Bern.

"Bon appetite," she said as she backed away.

Bern served them each a piece and Jenna folded the slice to lift it to her mouth, dripping with cheese and piping hot. *Oh my God, what could be better?* She closed her eyes in bliss as she bit into the delicious feast. The spices rolled around on her tongue, blending together in a symphony of epicurean delight.

She was savoring her single bite, chewing slowly and enjoying the flavor and texture. When she opened her eyes, Bern had devoured three pieces already. "Did you even taste it?" she asked.

"Of, course I did. I told you I was hungry."

Jenna laughed. "Yes, you did."

"Besides, if I slowed down to watch you eat, I would have come in my pants like a horny teenager. Good God woman, are you eating that pizza or making love to it?"

Jenna shrugged her shoulders. "I like pizza."

Bern growled. "Next time we're eating it at home, and I'll be licking it off your body," he said with a leer.

Jenna could feel herself blush, damn all she did was blush since she met this man. She looked down at the table. He reached across the table and lifted her chin. "Don't hide from me, little one. I love you, and there is nothing to be embarrassed about."

Seriously? All the times they'd made love together and he picks the middle of a pizza parlor to tell her he loves her for the first time? Did he really mean it? Maybe it was a good thing he was saying it when they weren't in the throes of passion. Maybe that meant he really did mean it. Should she say it back? Did she love him? Yeah, she did. She would never have agreed to the mating if she didn't, but somehow she just didn't feel right about telling him here and now.

She looked back at him and hoped the love she felt was conveyed in her eyes. She wasn't ready to voice it yet. It was too new, too fragile and she was scared. She really needed to get her shit together and put her big girl panties on. She wouldn't hurt Bern for anything, but she needed time. All of this was just happening so fast.

A brief flash of disappointment seemed to cross Bern's features, but it was gone so quickly she couldn't be sure she'd even seen it. Then he leaned across the table and lightly brushed her lips with a kiss.

She caressed his bearded cheek, God she loved his facial hair, he leaned into her hand.

"Let's finish eating and head for home," he said.

They finished their meal quickly. Chatting about the town, Bern's responsibilities to the clan and the students in Jenna's class. She told him some funny stories about the happenings in kindergarten and he told her about the inner circle of the clan, Martin, Guiles and Hans.

Maria said her goodbyes, gifting Jenna with a kiss to both cheeks this time as well as Bern and they sped off in the little sports car toward Jenna's house.

Jenna wasn't quite sure what to do when they reached her house. She'd never been in a relationship before, what was the protocol? They'd already had sex, twice today, should she invite him in to stay the night? She stifled a yawn as they pulled into the driveway.

Bern made the decision for her. He walked her to the door and asked for her keys, checked the house as he'd done on the previous occasion and came back to the front door. Handing her the keys he embraced her tenderly and kissed her like she was the most cherished thing on earth.

"Good night, little one. Sleep well and dream of me," he said and then he kissed her forehead and vaulted down the porch steps, waving goodbye as he sped away in the little sports car. Jenna touched her lips as she stood on the porch and watched him drive away. "Mine," the voice in her head said again. "Yes, ours," Jenna said out loud, with a smile and turned to go inside the house.

Jenna went to the bedroom and changed into her most comfortable sleep shirt and big fuzzy slippers. She went to the kitchen and made herself a cup of instant cocoa, with marshmallows, of course, and then she pulled the cordless phone from the wall and curled up in the corner of the sofa to dial Alice.

Her friend picked up on the second ring, as per usual no salutation for the Chicago girl, she just jumped right in. "Okay, so what's the update? Are you boinking like bunnies?"

"God, I needed to hear your voice."

"Why? What's the matter?" Alice was all business now.

"Nothing is the matter." Jenna sighed. "Everything is wonderful. It's just all happening so fast."

"Ooh, wonderful? I like wonderful. Dish. What's wonderful? Did you do the down and dirty?"

"You are such a slut. Yes, we had sex."

"And it was wonderful?"

"I fucking fainted!"

"You're shitting me? The first time?"

"No... When he marked me."

"Holy crap on a cracker. You're marked already? That means you're mated, right? Like forever and always?"

"Yep, forever and always," Jenna squeaked.

"You're freaking out."

"Yeah, kinda."

"What's wrong?"

"Nothing, everything. I don't know. I'm just scared. I've never even had a boyfriend and it's all happening so fast. He told me he loves me tonight."

"Well, that's good isn't it? Wait, you didn't say it back did you?"

"No," Jenna said miserably.

"But, you do don't you? Love him I mean."

"Yes, of course I do."

"So why didn't you tell him?"

"I don't know," Jenna whined. "Because I'm a stupid idiot."

"Hey! Only I'm allowed to call you a stupid idiot, you quit that."

"I need you."

"I figured."

"You did?"

"Yeah, I knew you'd be calling. I already put in for vacation. I'll be there on Saturday morning."

Jenna jumped off the couch and screamed. "You are the bestest best friend ever!"

"You better not let Beverly hear you say that."

"Oh my God, Bev, I haven't even called her."

"I called and let her know what's going on. She's tied up at some big convention, but she said she'd be there for the wedding."

"Wedding? Oh my God, I hadn't even thought about a wedding."

"Well, I know a mating is forever and all, but I assume your parents are going to want the traditional white wedding and all."

"Crap, you're right. How do I bring that up to Bern? It's not like I can just ask him to marry me."

"Leave that up to ole Alice, here. If he doesn't bring it up while I'm there I'll subtly bring it into the conversation."

"Subtly? You haven't been subtle about anything in your life."

"Well, there's a first time for everything." Alice laughed.

"Hey, bring a fancy dress with you. Bern and I have been invited to dinner with the alpha of the neighboring wolf clan on Saturday. It's a big friggin' deal."

"Are you sure it's okay for you to just bring someone with you?"

"I don't think it will be a problem, Bern is bringing several guards with us, you can be one of the guard's dates or something."

"Okay, if you're sure."

"I'm sure. I can't wait for you to get here. I'm so excited. God, I miss you girl. I wish I could hug you through the phone."

"It's only a few days until Saturday, and then I'll hug the stuffing out of you. Can you hold out until then?"

"I'll have to, won't I?"

"Yes, you will. I gotta go. Love you, girl!"

"Love you too, see you Saturday."

Jenna danced around in a circle before she hung up the phone. Alice was coming!

Chapter Eight

Bern was knocking at her door at seven o'clock the next morning. Jenna couldn't wait to tell him her news, she threw open the door and jumped into his arms. She hooked her legs around his waist and he supported her butt with his arms.

"Well good morning. Someone's in a good mood today."

"Guess what?"

"What?"

"I called Alice last night and she's coming to visit! She'll be here Saturday."

"Wonderful."

"Is it okay if she comes to Von Drake's with us, because I kind of already told her it was," she said all in one breath.

Bern laughed, "Yes, it should be fine, I'll send Bastian a note to inform him your friend will be in town and joining us."

"He won't be mad will he?" Jenna asked.

"No, it will actually be a nice ice breaker. Help lessen the tension."

"Oh good, I can't wait for you to meet Alice." Jenna gave him a big squeeze and dropped her legs. Bern let her slowly slide down the front of his body. Somebody was very happy to see her too.

Hans stepped up to the front gate and cleared his throat.

Bern stepped back. "Good morning, Hans. Would you like to walk with us today?"

"*Ja, Sippe.*"

"Do you mind, Jenna? Hans was on a reconnaissance mission last night and I need his report."

"No, that's fine. If you need to work, I'm more than capable of walking to school alone."

Bern gave her a stern look. "No, you are not. You are to go nowhere alone. Do you understand me?"

Jenna clicked her heels together and saluted. "Yes, sir."

Bern slapped her butt. "Impertinent cub, I may have to punish you later," he teased with a waggle of his eyebrows.

Bern linked their hands and Hans fell into step beside them as they struck out for the school.

"So, what did you discover, my friend?" Bern asked.

"Nothing decisive, I'm afraid, *Sippe*. As Boyd said, five men are camped about ten miles outside town. They have fishing equipment with them and there were fresh fish at the camp, but I also saw several rifles and tranquilizer guns.

It's possible they are just cautious and prepared in case they run into an animal in the wild. I listened around the camp, but they weren't talking about anything but fishing. Sorry."

"Nothing to be sorry about. That's what reconnaissance is about. Learning what we can. Let's add the camp to our nightly patrols. Keep an eye on it, make sure these men aren't up to no good."

"*Ja, Sippe.*"

"What's going on?" Jenna asked.

"Nothing to worry about. Just making sure that some campers are just campers and not agents from HUNTS."

Jenna shivered. "God, I hate even hearing about that group. They're worse than the KKK. The news has reported some terrible things they've done. I don't understand why the government hasn't shut them down."

"There's always been hate groups against people who are different. The government can't shut them down unless they catch them in the act, and even then they can only arrest the people that are involved at the time."

"I don't understand it, why do they hate shifters?"

"I don't know, little one. Why do the KKK hate black people? Who can understand hate?"

Jenna rested her head on his shoulder and they walked in silence for the rest of the way to the school. When they reached the entrance Bern kissed her goodbye and Jenna went inside. Hans took up his post, hidden from view, but guarding Jenna from outside the school.

* * * *

At the end of the day Jenna's cell phone rang. "Hello," she answered.

"Hello, beautiful," Bern said. "I'm running a few minutes late, please wait for me at the school, okay?"

"Sure, no problem. Your sister is running late again too. I'm going to take Sarah out to play on the playground while we wait."

"Okay, I'll meet you there."

Jenna took Sarah by the hand and led her to the playground. She set her purse and tote bag on a bench, along with Sarah's backpack and took Sarah over to the swing set. Hans sat on the bench in the shade and watched Jenna push Sarah on the swings.

Jenna's heightened senses weren't enough for her to notice the scent of the humans that lurked in the shadows of the woods adjacent to the playground. Three men watched the human push the bear cub on the swings with covetous eyes.

Arms reached around Jenna's middle and she shrieked, elbowing the body behind her. Bern grunted. "Hey, that's not very nice."

"You scared the crap out of me! Sneaky bear!"

"Unca Bern," Sarah screamed and launched herself at her uncle's legs.

"Hello, munchkin," he said tossing her in the air and giving her Eskimo kisses. "How's my girl today?"

"Okay," she said with a sigh, "'cept, Mommy's late again."

"Mommy got tied up, so uncle Bern's gonna take you home. Is that okay?"

Sarah smiled like she'd won the prize at the county fair. "Really? Yeah! Are we going to your house?"

"No, we're going home to your house, but I thought maybe we'd stop for ice cream first," Bern said.

"Yippee!" Sarah hollered.

"Now I see why you're her favorite Unca," Jenna said and bumped shoulders with Bern.

"You bet, little one. I gotta earn points where I can. You up for some ice cream?"

"Always," Jenna said.

The three of them walked hand in hand to the ice cream parlor and got double scoops. Jenna got triple chocolate fudge, Sarah got cookies and cream and Bern got maple walnut crunch. They sat at the cute little wrought iron tables outside the ice cream parlor devouring their confections.

Sarah seemed to have more on her face than she managed to get in her mouth. Thankfully, Bern had grabbed a stack of napkins from the counter. "Come here, sweetie," Jenna said as she grabbed a napkin and tried to halt the flow of ice cream before it dripped onto Sarah's T-shirt.

"I can see you doing that with a child of ours one day soon," Bern said.

Jenna laughed. "That's funny, I was thinking the same thing the other day when you were holding Jimmy."

Bern raised a brow. "Oh, it's something we haven't talked about, but I'm glad to hear you say that. I want children. Our children."

Jenna swallowed, he looked at her with such love in his eyes. "I do too. I want a little boy with your big brown eyes."

Bern reached forward and cupped her chin. "I want a little girl with your beautiful blonde curls." He leaned in and kissed her over Sarah's head.

Sarah put a hand on each of their chests and pushed them apart. "Quit it, you're squishing me."

They both laughed, the moment broken. Bern tousled her hair. "Okay, munchkin, are you finished with your ice cream?" A soggy piece of cone was all that remained of Sarah's treat.

"Yes, I'm done."

Bern wrapped the mess in another napkin and tossed it in a nearby trash can. "I think we should go inside and wash up before we head to Sarah's house," Jenna said.

"Good idea," Bern said. Jenna took Sarah inside to wash up, while Bern took out his cell phone and placed a call. Jenna assumed he was calling Julia to let her know they were on their way.

Bern was off the phone when Jenna and Sarah returned to his side. Sarah took up a position between them skipping and swinging her hands as the three made their way across town. Sarah talked non-stop, telling Jenna all about the family.

She learned the names of all Bern's sisters, Julia, Andrea, Dagmar, Sofie and Hannah. Sarah also recited the names of all eleven of her cousins, but Jenna wasn't about to try and memorize all those names. She did manage to catch the three in Sarah's family, she already knew about Jimmy and then there was an older boy named Nicholas.

Sarah's prattle left Jenna free to think, her mind kept drifting back to Bern and the soft loving look he had given her at the restaurant. The big bear was nothing but a softie at heart. They turned onto the walkway of a cute little ranch style home and were just nearing the door when a hellacious roar sounded from behind the closed door.

Jenna stopped in her tracks and Sarah smirked. "Uh oh, Mommy's mad," Sarah said in a singsong voice.

Bern stopped and looked down at Jenna and Sarah. "You'd better stay here and let me see what's going on," he said, he pushed her toward some chairs on the front porch and cautiously approached the front door.

"Better watch out, Unca Bern, Mommy throws things when she's mad," Sarah warned a bit late, as a vase sailed past Bern's head through the open doorway.

"Yes, I remember," Bern muttered. "Julia!" he called. A roar answered his call and Bern's eyes shifted from brown to gold, his teeth elongated in his mouth and Jenna was shocked by the roar that emanated from his mouth. Silence followed.

No more projectiles came toward the door and Bern entered the now quiet interior. Jenna heard some scuffling and what sounded like moving of furniture and then low harsh voices. Finally Bern reappeared on the porch followed by a red-faced Julia.

"I'm so sorry, Jenna. I was having a…moment." Julia said self-consciously.

"You were mad," Sarah said.

"Um, yes," Julia said. "Again, sorry." Julia blushed furiously. "You shouldn't get between a bear and her chocolate when she's PMSing."

Jenna laughed. "Well, it's a good thing to know some things are the same whether bear or human. I may not be able to roar that loud, but I sure have wanted to in the past."

Julia laughed and just like that they bonded in the way of women. PMS was the universal bond.

"Please come in, I promise not to bite you. I'll even make some coffee. Just don't eat my chocolate."

"I promise, Scout's honor. We just had ice cream anyway and I had triple chocolate fudge."

"And you didn't bring me any? Strike that, I may have to kill you now."

Julia led them into a large country kitchen, Jimmy sat in a high chair at the table, Cheerios sprinkled across the tray, a huge man in a blue work shirt and khaki pants sat at the table reading the newspaper.

"Jenna, this is my husband James," Julia said. James stood and extended a large paw to shake with her.

"Um, hi," he said. "Sorry, about the noise when you arrived. Jules was feeling a little grumbly."

Jenna laughed. "So we heard."

"Have a seat," James said, indicating a chair at the table. Bern held a chair out and seated her and then straddled one for himself. Sarah climbed into her daddy's lap and kissed his cheek.

"Hi, Daddy. I got to swing and have ice cream," she said.

"That's great, pumpkin. Were you a good girl for Uncle Bern?"

"Course I was, I's always a good girl," Sarah said, and Jenna swore she could almost see the little girl twisting her father around her little fingers. Sarah was definitely Daddy's girl.

James kissed her nose and patted her behind setting her down on the floor. "Why don't you go up to your room and get washed up for dinner?"

"Okay, Daddy," she said with another kiss to his cheek, she skipped off to the other room. James' gaze followed her out of the room before it turned to Bern and Jenna.

"I hear congratulations are in order. 'Bout time you finally mated old man," James said.

"Don't you start now too," Bern said.

"Oh, come on, what's the fun of being the *Sippe*'s brother-in-law if I can't give you a hard time?"

"I get enough of that from my infernal sisters."

"That's the truth. Meddling bunch of sows," James muttered, only to be smacked in the back of the head by his wife, who growled menacingly.

"Children," Bern rumbled.

"Don't you children me, Bern Allen, I'm older than you are."

"Doesn't matter, *schwester* mine, I am your *Sippe*."

"Yeah, and you never let me forget it either." Julia laughed.

Julia set cups of coffee in front of each of them, along with cream and sugar, then took a seat across the table from Jenna. "Since you're here, I don't have to call you about dinner. I talked to all my sisters and everyone can make it on Wednesday, does that work for you?"

"My friend Alice is coming into town this weekend, but if you don't mind her joining us, that's fine. Where do you want to have dinner? Here?"

"No, at Bern's house of course."

Jenna was taken aback for a moment, they invited her to dinner, did they expect her to cook? She looked at Bern, "Um, at your house? Are you cooking?"

"I could, but no. Julia extended the invitation, so she gets to plan the meal."

"Oh, don't worry about that. All the girls will bring something. We've got it covered."

"Okay. Would you like me to make something? I could make dessert. I make a mean honey cake."

"Ooh, that sounds great! I love honey cake."

"Maybe I'll actually get to make it this time. I've been trying to make one for the last week and *something* keeps getting in the way," she said with a sassy wink at Bern.

He waggled his eyebrows at her. "I can't help it if I have better things for you to do with your time than bake," he teased.

They finished their coffee and Jenna received a hug and kiss goodbye from Bern's sister. She could already tell they were going to be good friends. Julia held her just that extra second longer when they hugged, the extra squeeze that said, this isn't because it's what I'm supposed to do, but because I care for you.

Jenna exited Julia's house with a smile on her face, hand linked with Bern's and swinging them between them as they walked. She was high on life and walking on air.

The trip back to Jenna's house was short and this time Jenna had no doubt what was going to happen when they got there. Bern would be spending the night, because she was hotter than hell and she was going to jump his bones the minute they walked through the door.

Between his awesome sweetness with Sarah and his growly gruffness with his sister, Jenna's motor was revving in high speed. Every step they walked closer to her house was torture. Her nipples were straining against her bra, and her panties were beyond damp. Damn, Bern needed to hurry up and get her home or she was going to attack him right here on the street.

She took a deep breath, trying to calm her raging libido and instead the delicious scent her newly awakened senses detected as Bern assaulted her nostrils. She leaned her head onto his shoulder, seeking more of the alluring fragrance, a low growl crawled up from her throat. "Mine." The voice in her head murmured. *Yes, I know*, she answered it in her thoughts.

Bern stopped and looked down at her. "Are you all right?"

She looked up at him through her lashes, and then nuzzled his neck. "Mmm, you smell so good."

Bern took her by the shoulders and pulled her away from his body. He looked into her eyes.

"Um, Jenna, your eyes are amber."

That snapped Jenna out of her trance, "What?"

"Little one, I don't know what's going on, but you seem to be changing much faster than normal. Your bear is coming through already and it's only been a day. The full moon is still weeks away. I've never heard of this happening before. The way you're acting…it's almost like you're going into heat."

"I beg your pardon, I may be a little horny, but you don't have to be rude about it."

"I'm not being rude, little one, and believe me, I certainly don't mind you being horny, but it seems like more than that."

"Maybe," she muttered, burying her face in his chest, mortified by her behavior.

Bern tipped her chin up and looked down into her face, he kissed her nose and then gently, tenderly kissed her lips. "Don't be embarrassed, please, my little one. I love that you want me. I want you too. Oh so much." He kissed her again with such passion Jenna felt fire unfurl in her belly.

"Let's go home," she said.

Bern wrapped his arm around her shoulders and held her close as they finished the short journey to her house. As she stood on the front porch waiting for him to check the house Jenna paced, she really was in need. She needed Bern in her arms, his warmth, his strength, his passion.

Bern returned to the front door and pulled Jenna inside, before the door had even closed behind them she was in his arms. He carried her straight to the bedroom and a trail of their clothes littered the floor along the way. By the time they reached the bed they were both naked.

No foreplay was necessary, Jenna was wet and ready, she needed her big bear inside her. "Hurry Bern, I need you," she pleaded.

Bern lay down on the bed and pulled Jenna on top of him. "Ride me, little one. You control the pace."

Jenna reached between them and grasped Bern's rigid cock. She placed the head against her opening and slid it back and forth, coating him in moisture. His tip bumped her clit and she shuddered, God, it felt so good, she did it again. Then she began to take him inside, slowly lowering herself onto his thick shaft. She'd never been on top before and he felt bigger this way, so full, so deep.

She braced her hand on his chest for leverage, massaging his pecs and rubbing her hands against the hair as she began to move her hips. Oh man this was good, she ground her hips in a circle, her clit dragged across the hair on Bern's pelvis and an electric shiver shot up Jenna's spine.

Bern placed his hands on her hips, helping to support her and guiding her movements. Jenna lifted her hips and dropped back down, faster and faster, rotating and grinding on the downward thrust. She was in a frenzy, panting and calling Bern's name, her nails scoring his chest.

Bern growled deep and thrust his hips up to meet hers, Jenna cried out, pleading for release. Bern reached between them and thrummed her clit, flicking and teasing until she finally came in a burst of white light behind her closed eyelids.

Bern followed a few thrusts later, spilling his hot cum inside her spasming channel. Jenna collapsed on his rib cage, their sweat soaked bodies sticking together and she rested her head on his heaving chest. His arms came around her and he rolled them to their sides.

Bern kissed her eyelids, forehead and hairline as their breathing returned to normal. "I love you, little one," he whispered.

This time Jenna wasn't stupid enough to not return the sentiment, she looked deep into his chocolate eyes. "I love you too, my big bear," she said, and kissed him long and passionately.

Chapter Nine

The rest of the week passed quickly and before Jenna knew it Saturday morning had arrived. She and Bern were sitting at the kitchen table drinking coffee when a knock sounded at the door. Jenna squealed and raced for the door. She threw it open and launched herself at her unsuspecting friend.

Poor Alice barely managed to stay on her feet when five foot ten inches of overexcited female grabbed her in a ferocious hug. "I'm so glad you're here," Jenna gushed, pulling back and kissing both Alice's cheeks. "You look fabulous. Come inside. Bern will get your bags," she said as she pulled Alice toward the kitchen.

Alice looked shell shocked, Jenna should take a picture, because that never happened. Bern stepped into view and Alice's eyes widened. She gazed from Bern's feet up, up, up to his face, then looked at Jenna and mouthed, "Wow."

Jenna beamed. "Bern sweetie, will you get Alice's bags, she left them on the porch. Can you put them in the spare room, please?"

"Sure, little one." Bern went to the porch and behind his back Alice fanned her face. "Oh my," she whispered.

"I know, right," Jenna giggled. She linked arms with her friend and led her into the kitchen. Jenna pushed Alice onto a chair at the kitchen table and poured her a cup of coffee. Then she sat and faced her friend taking both of her hands in her own.

"I'm so glad you're here. I've missed you so much. How long are you going to be able to stay?"

"Just the week, But including the weekends on both sides that gives us nine days."

Jenna squeezed her hands. "That's wonderful. We'll get to have such a good visit. I can't wait for you to get to know Bern. Oh, Al, he is…amazing."

"You look so happy, Jenna. You're absolutely glowing."

"I know, I feel like I'm walking on air, and I'm so excited about tonight. Did you bring a fabulous dress? I really want to impress Bastian Von Drake."

"Who is this guy?"

"He's the alpha of the neighboring wolf pack. It's a big deal that he invited us to dinner. Very formal. Ritzy. He and Bern are kind of frenimies."

"Oh, what exactly does that mean?"

"They get along on the surface, but there is all kinds of underlying politics and shit. I don't understand it all, but it's important that we make a good impression."

"Is he as cute as Bern?"

"I don't know." Jenna laughed. "I doubt it, no one is as cute as my Bern."

"Oh, you've got it so bad girl," Alice teased.

Bern chose that moment to return to the room. Jenna could feel the blush color her cheeks. Bern brushed her hot cheek with the back of his hand. "What are you up to, little one that has you blushing so sweetly?"

"Nothing, girl talk."

"Mm-hmm, I'll bet." Bern turned to Alice. "We didn't get properly introduced. I am Bern Allen Helms." He took her hand and kissed the knuckles.

"Alice Miller. Nice to finally meet you. Jenna has been singing your praises."

Bern gave Jenna a heated look. "Have you been kissing and telling my sweet?"

Alice burst out laughing. "You can't ask that."

Bern looked at her startled. "I can't?"

"Nope, it's against the girl code."

"Girl code?"

"Yep, men are not allowed to know what best friends talk about. That's the girl code."

"Oh really. Does the same apply for men? Am I allowed to have secrets with my men friends?"

"Of course not," Alice and Jenna said together.

"Well now, that doesn't seem fair," Bern replied.

Alice and Jenna laughed. "Nobody ever said life was fair," Alice said.

Bern laughed. "No, that's true."

He turned to Jenna. "I'm sorry, little one, but I need to get going. I have some work I need to get done before tonight."

Jenna leaned up and kissed him. "That's okay, we have a ton of catching up to do and it will take us half the day to get ready for tonight," Jenna said with a smile.

"We'll be here to pick you up at six."

"We'll be ready."

Bern pulled her close and kissed her deeply. "Until then, little one."

Alice and Jenna spent the morning on the couch, drinking coffee and catching up on each other's lives. Jenna had little to talk about besides Bern, he seemed to have taken over her life, even though they'd only known each other a week. It hardly seemed possible that they had been together that short a time. It felt like she'd known him forever.

Alice on the other hand droned on and on about her job. She was a career girl down to her toes. She was working at a prominent advertising agency in Chicago and had just landed a plumb account. It looked like a promotion was on the horizon and she was over the moon.

Jenna glanced at the clock, it was almost noon. "We'd better start getting ready. I get the shower first!" she called, jumping up and rushing for the stairs. Since there was no fancy salon in Honey Corners, the girls had decided to do each other's hair and makeup. It would be just like when they were back in college.

Jenna took her time in the shower, shaving every inch of exposed skin and exfoliating with her body scrub. She shampooed and used a deep conditioner on her hair and then rinsed all the lather down the drain, finishing with a cold spray to close her pores.

Shivering, she jumped from the shower and briskly toweled herself off, lightly spraying her skin with Channel body satin spray, it smelled divine and left her soft and silky. Wrapping the bath sheet around herself, she quickly finger dried her hair with the blow dryer, and plugged in her hot rollers.

She rummaged in her vanity for her nail polish case, it was practically a suitcase. She was kind of a nail polish whore. She carried the case out into her bedroom to find Alice laying on her bed.

"'Bout time you got out of there. I was about to send in the SEALs for a rescue mission."

Jenna laughed.

"Did you leave me any hot water, bitch?" Alice griped.

"I have a tankless water heater."

"Damn, that rocks." Alice high fived her on the way to the bathroom. "If I don't come out in an hour, send in the SEALs," she said with a wink.

"I'll get right on that, but I don't know if we have any seal shifters in town. How about a wolf or a bear?"

"Ha ha, you are so funny. Not." Alice slammed the bathroom door behind her, and Jenna fell on the bed laughing hysterically.

Once her mirth subsided she stood up and dropped the towel on a chair and slipped into a silky robe. She padded to the closet and pulled her dress for the evening. She hung it on the closet door and stared at the glorious creation.

Jenna had prowled the internet and been so lucky to find the perfect dress and have it delivered in time for the dinner. It was a deep emerald green, empire waisted, halter dress, the skirt was full and flowing, chiffon. It was so beautiful. She had an adorable pair of sparkly silver peek toe pumps to go with it, and squee, she got to wear heels! For once, she could wear a heeled shoe and not be taller than her date.

Plucking the dress from the door she held it front of her and danced around the room. She caught sight of herself in the dressing table mirror and stalled, was that girl really her? The deep green of the dress set off her cream colored skin beautifully, and her eyes shone like emeralds in the night sky. She looked…glowing, effervescent, happy.

She stared at her reflection in the mirror and smiled dreamily, all her dreams were coming true. She was the luckiest girl in the world. Tears threatened, but she blinked them back, turning and placing the dress back on the closet door.

The bathroom door opened emitting a burst of steam into the room. "Hot damn, that shower is amazing," Alice said. "I'm moving in."

Jenna laughed. "I wish you were serious, that would be the second best news of my life."

Alice walked over and hugged her. "Well, I would if I could, but you know I'm a Chi-town girl. I don't think I'd ever leave Chicago, except maybe for New York. I'm city all the way, babe."

Jenna kissed her cheek. "I know, I know. You have green beer in your veins, and Polish sausage in your heart."

"You got that right!" Alice chortled. "Speaking of, I'm starving. You got some food around this joint?"

"Are you kidding me? Who are you talking to, girl? I'll go make us some sandwiches. You get out your dress and find a nail polish to match it while I do. Okay?"

"Gotcha."

Jenna jogged down to the kitchen and made them some sub sandwiches, grabbed a bag of chips, a couple of cokes and headed back up the stairs. She wondered what Alice's dress would look like. In college everyone called them Mutt and Jeff, because as big as Jenna was, Alice was tiny, five foot two inches tall, one hundred and ten pounds, soaking wet. Alice only had two big things on her body, well I guess you would say three, her mouth and her boobs.

She was not anatomically correct. The boob fairy had given her a double dose, she had a tiny waist, tiny hips, tiny feet, tiny everything, and huge knockers. She always looked like she was about to fall over. While Alice had the most beautiful big cornflower blue eyes you ever saw, men never looked at her face, they stared at her chest.

Jenna pushed into the bedroom balancing the sandwiches on two plates, she had the chips hanging from one hand and the sodas in the pockets of her robe. "Room service," she called.

"Yum." Alice plopped onto the bed. "Bring it over here girl."

Jenna crossed to the bed and saw Alice's dress hanging next to her own. It was a strapless silver sheath, with sequined accents at the waist and bodice. The color would look fabulous with Alice's blonde hair and blue eyes.

"Oh, your dress is beautiful," Jenna said.

"Thanks, yours is fab too. Where did you get it?"

"Internet."

"Awesome."

The girls were quiet for a few minutes as they wolfed down their sandwiches and drinks.

Four hours later Alice and Jenna were finally ready. Toes and fingernails painted. Jenna's hair fixed in an elegant French twist, with tiny curls framing her face. Alice's short hair bounced in soft waves around her pixie features. Both had perfectly applied makeup and they sat in Jenna's living room sipping a glass of wine and waiting for Bern to arrive.

At six o'clock on the dot a knock sounded at the door. Jenna opened it to be stunned breathless. Bern stood on the doorstep decked out in a black tuxedo, a tall handsome gentleman at his side. He leaned in and kissed her cheek, then took her hand and kissed her palm. "You look beautiful my little one."

"Thank you," she mumbled, almost incapable of speech. "Come in, we need to get our coats."

Alice had come to stand behind her.

"Let me introduce my friend, and second, Martin Kramer. Martin, this is Jenna Raynes, my mate, and her friend, Alice Miller."

Martin nodded and extended a hand to Jenna. "We have met before, Miss Raynes, at your interview with the school board, but it is a pleasure to see you again," Martin said.

"Please call me Jenna."

Martin nodded and kissed her knuckles, he then turned to Alice. "Miss Miller, pleased to meet you."

"Since you're supposed to be my date for tonight, I think you can call me Alice," she teased.

Martin kissed her fingers. "As you wish, my lady, Alice."

Alice giggled. "Oh this is gonna be fun!"

"We best get going," Bern said. "Where is your wrap?"

Jenna had placed her black rabbit jacket over the chair in the foyer, it had been a graduation gift from her father and she loved the coat. She picked it up and Bern plucked it from her hand and held it for her while she slipped her arms into the sleeves.

Martin had done the same for Alice and the four strolled out the front door. As Bern was checking to make sure the door locked behind them, Jenna stared in shock at the limousine that sat perched in her driveway. Holy shit! She knew this was a fancy dinner, but she didn't know it was this fancy.

Bern led her to the door of the limo, where Hans acted as chauffeur and held the door open awaiting their entrance. They pulled out into the street and Jenna noticed three dark SUVs following them. "Are those your guards?" she asked.

"Yes, those are my men."

"How many are coming with us?"

"Only ten."

"Ten? That seems like an awful lot."

"Not really. It is a small contingent when going into another's territory."

Jenna raised an eyebrow. "If you say so."

Bern kissed her. "I do."

She shrugged her shoulders. "Okay."

Alice leaned forward and tapped Jenna on the shoulder. "Everything okay?"

"Yep, everything is *peachy*."

"Uh-huh," Alice murmured. Everything is peachy was code for something's up but I can't talk about it, or don't want to talk about it. The girls had used it for years, so Alice now knew something was up.

Martin tried to make small talk, but the atmosphere in the limousine was strained and he finally gave up. They rode the remaining fifteen minutes in virtual silence. Bern held Jenna's hand and gently stroked her knuckles, trying to soothe her agitation. She should tell him it wasn't working.

After what seemed like forever they pulled into a long tree lined drive. A huge plantation style house sat at the end of the drive. As soon as the limousine stopped a uniformed attendant opened the car door and extended a hand to assist Jenna out. Bern growled. Jenna ignored him and exited the limo.

She stood quietly on the sidewalk as Alice climbed out, followed by Martin and Bern. A tall dark man stood in the open doorway to the house. He was backlit, so Jenna could not see his features, but he exuded power and strength. This had to be Bastian Von Drake, the alpha.

Bern placed his hand at the small of her back and guided her toward the door, Martin and Alice followed. The man stepped forward and extended his hand. "Good evening, *Sippe* Helms. How good of you to come."

Bern clasped his hand and nodded. "Good evening, Alpha Von Drake. I thank you for your kind invitation. May I present my mate, Jenna Raynes, her friend, Alice Miller, and you know my second, Martin Kruger of course?"

A strange scent suddenly filled the air and Jenna could have sworn the alpha wolf's eyes flashed amber for a moment, but he closed them briefly and when he opened them they were the normal dark brown they had been before. She blinked, wondering if she had imagined the whole thing. She tried to catch Bern's attention, but all his concentration was on the alpha.

"Sebastian Von Drake," he said with a slight bow, leaning down to kiss Jenna's hand, he repeated the gesture with Alice. Then turned her hand over and kissed Alice's palm, did she imagine it or did he sniff Alice's wrist? What the hell was going on?

He briefly shook Martin's hand and turned on his heel. "Come, let's adjourn to the library for a drink before dinner."

Alice leaned into Jenna's ear and whispered. "What bug crawled up his ass?"

Bern cleared his throat loudly, and whispered back. "Shifters have very good hearing."

Alice covered her mouth with her hand and then mouthed, *Sorry, my bad.*

Bastian's back was ramrod straight as he led the way to the library. He gave no indication he had heard Alice's remark. He paused at an open doorway and gestured for them to enter. Bern stepped back allowing Jenna to enter before him, and then followed her into the darkly paneled room.

Heavy leather furniture filled the center of a room surrounded by bookshelves filled with tomes. Everything from modern day spy novels to rare historic manuscripts filled the shelves. Jenna could go crazy in here.

"What a lovely room," she remarked.

"Thank you, my dear." Bastian replied. "What can I get you to drink? Wine, or something stronger?"

"Wine would be lovely," Jenna said.

"Wine for me also," Alice replied.

"Whiskey, on the rocks, for me, thanks," said Bern.

"I'll have the same," Martin said.

The four of them chose seats around the room. Jenna and Bern on the sofa. Alice on the loveseat and Martin in the arm chair across from her. Bastian uncorked a bottle of wine and brought it and three glasses to the table, he left the wine to breathe while he fixed Bern and Martin their whiskeys.

He handed the men their drinks and proceeded to pour a tiny sip of wine into a glass, he swirled the liquid around, held it to the light and then handed it to Alice. He bowed again. "For your pleasure, my lady."

Alice looked at Jenna and cocked an eyebrow in a *what the hell question*. Jenna shrugged and mouthed *just go with it*. Alice tipped the glass to her lips and swallowed the small sample.

"Delicious," she said.

Bastian beamed and filled the three glasses handing one to Jenna and Alice and keeping the last for himself, he sat next to Alice on the love seat. Jenna watched as he closed his eyes and took a deep breath.

"So Bastian, while I appreciate the invitation. I'm curious as to what prompted it. You have never invited me to your home before," Bern said.

"I heard of your good fortune and wished to meet your mate. Is that not reason enough?" Bastian asked.

"I suppose, but tell me, how did you hear of my mating? I had barely announced it to my clan when I received your invitation, and how did your wolf come into my territory undetected?"

"Come now, Bern. This is not the time to talk of such things. We are in the company of two beautiful women, politics can wait until we are alone," he said sternly. "We will talk after dinner, I have some things to discuss with you, for now let us enjoy ourselves."

Jenna could feel the tension radiating off of Bern, but he controlled it and pulled back. "You're right, my friend. Let's take this time to get to know each other better. You come from Russia, yes?"

"Yes, though I have been in the United Stated for over four hundred years."

Alice gasped. "Four hundred years? How the hell old are you?"

Bastian looked down his patrician nose at her. "I am five hundred fifty-seven years of age."

"Holy shit! I didn't know you guys lived that long." She turned to Jenna. "Did you know shifters lived that long? What the hell? You're gonna get old and wrinkly and Bern's still gonna look like that. How the hell is that going to work?"

Jenna could feel the blush crawl across her face. What the hell was she supposed to say? Bern said she wasn't allowed to tell anyone. Not even Alice.

Bastian took the dilemma from her hands. "It is not common knowledge, but shifters can change their mates. Once a shifter claims and bites his mate, she turns, becomes a shifter like him."

Alice's eyes practically bugged out of her head. "You didn't fucking tell me that!" she yelled at Jenna.

"Um, sorry. I was told I couldn't. It wasn't allowed." Jenna looked at Bern. "What's going on? Why did he tell her?"

"I'm not sure. Bastian?"

Bastian took both of Alice's hands in his. "I told you because you need to know, krasivaya—beautiful—because you are mine. You are my mate."

"Shut the fuck up," Alice burst out.

Bastian did not look amused. "It is true, sweet Alice. I knew the moment we met."

"Look, I get you shifters have this whole, I sniff you, you're my mate thing, and it works for you. It worked great for Jenna. She's super happy and I'm glad for her, but I'm not interested. I have a career I've been busting my ass for. I'm up for a big promotion, I just signed a new client. I'm leaving in eight days. So you can just go sniff somebody else's tree."

"It doesn't work that way Alice. It is a rare and wonderful thing to meet one's mate. I never thought to be lucky enough to meet a second mate in my lifetime."

"You already have a mate? Well see there, then you don't need me."

Bastian's eyes filled with sadness. "I had a mate, in Russia, four hundred years ago. She was killed, along with my unborn child. I thought I would be alone for the rest of my years."

Jenna saw Alice's tough veneer crack for just a moment, but she quickly shored it up. "I'm sorry for your loss, but really, I'm not interested in a relationship, and as I said. I'm leaving in a week."

Bastian nodded, but Jenna could see that he was only backing down to regroup. Alice may have won this battle, but she hadn't won the war. The alpha wasn't going to give up that easily.

A knock sounded at the library door. "Enter," Bastian called.

"Your other guests have arrived, Alpha, and dinner is ready to be served. Do you wish me to bring your guests into the library or will you be adjourning to the dining room, sir?" A suited gentleman asked from the doorway.

Bastian raised Alice's hand to his lips again and kissed her palm. "Are you ready to dine, my dear?" he asked, as if no one else was in the room. Alice frantically looked around the room, her eyes met Jenna's begging for help. Jenna shrugged her shoulders and flippantly waved her hand. Alice rolled her eyes and if looks could kill, Jenna would have been dead on the spot.

"Um, yeah, sure. Let's eat."

"Send the guests to the dining room, Bradley. We will join them there shortly."

"Very well, sir." Bradley turned on his heel and silently left the room. Bastian swallowed the last of his wine, his gaze still firmly fixed on Alice. He set his glass on the table and stood, extending his hand to help Alice from her seat. Once they were both standing he finally turned to the rest of his guests.

"Dinner awaits." He gestured toward the door and led the way, his hand gently guiding Alice by the waist. The group entered the dining room and Jenna stifled a gasp at the opulence. A table large enough to seat forty people was bedecked with a brilliant white linen table cloth and deep red napkins folded into fans at each place setting. Gold flatware, and crystal goblets edged in gold sat beside china plates ringed with gold, then red, and finally cream in the center.

What must be Russian tapestries, depicting scenes of wolves fighting men at war adorned the walls. The ceiling was at least twelve feet high, with exposed wooden beams crisscrossing the expanse of white stucco. The floor was black marble. In all, the room was breathtaking.

Over half the seats were filled. Jenna had wondered where Bern's guards had disappeared to while they were in the library. They were now at the dining room table, along with several men she had never met.

Bastian led the group to the head of the table. He seated Alice to the right hand side and Bern to the left of himself at the head. Jenna sat beside Bern, with Martin next to her. She recognized

Hers to Bear

Guiles and Hans and knew a few other of Bern's guards by sight, but not name.

Once everyone was seated Bastian began introductions. "Jenna, Alice, this is my second, Anton, and my lieutenant, Viktor. I will not burden you with introduction to all the guards, it would be too many names to try to remember. Bern, Martin, you have met before, yes?"

Bern and Martin nodded. Jenna and Alice exchanged greetings with the two men seated next to Alice. Both were tall and handsome with sharp eastern European features.

Two women brought out covered trays, they stopped beside Bastian's chair and uncovered the trays. "Sesame salmon croquettes, sir."

"Lovely, you may serve, my dears," he responded.

Jenna couldn't quite fathom how formal Bastian's household appeared to be, but when the succulent little morsels were set in front of her, she sighed in bliss. Oh this was going to be some meal.

The dinner was beyond belief. The appetizers were followed by beef consume, salad, beef wellington, with roasted potatoes and baby asparagus, a decadent chocolate mousse, and then a cheese platter. Jenna was well aware that her bear ate like…well a bear, but it appeared wolves were rather voracious too.

Even so, conversation flowed throughout the meal and Jenna was surprised when she looked at her watch to discover over two hours had passed while they consumed their meal.

"My dear ladies, would you mind terribly if Bern and I escaped to my office for a few moments of business talk? Martin and Anton can keep you company in the garden until we return."

Jenna nodded. "Of course, that's fine. Thank you so much for the wonderful dinner."

Bastian took her hand and kissed it. "My pleasure, my dear. Your company turned simple fare to an extraordinary experience." Bastian rose from the table. "Come, Bern." He turned without bothering to see if Bern followed, arrogant in his position and power.

Chapter Ten

Before Bastian could reach the door Anton jumped to his feet. "Alpha, do you not think Martin and I should join you?"

Bastian turned and gave his second a withering look. "No, I do not. If I felt you should join us, I would have included you in the invitation. Please take the ladies out to the patio and give them a tour of my lovely gardens. We will join you when *our* business is completed."

Bern felt the alpha's power surge through the room. It was palpable. *Damn, the were was strong.* Every head in the room, including those of his own guards bowed. Anton looked like he was going to swallow his tongue. Anger burned in his eyes, but they dropped to the floor.

"Yes, Alpha."

Bastian turned on his heel and left the room without another word or gesture. A man confident in his power. Bern followed, glad he wasn't on the bad side of this wolf. They didn't return to the library, but headed right down the long hallway, stopping at a small office, much like Bern's own private space.

Bastian closed and locked the door behind them. He indicated a plush leather chair in front of the desk and walked over to a built in bar along the wall. "Cognac?" he asked.

Bern nodded and he poured a small amount into two snifters and swirled the liquid, staring into the glasses. He turned and brought one to Bern, perching on the edge of his desk. "I know you must be curious as to why I asked you here."

"I'll admit, my curiosity is piqued."

"I have been watching you, Bern. Now, don't go getting your hackles up. I don't mean spying on you. I mean observing you from afar. Watching your style of leadership. I think you are a good man. A good bear."

While Bern didn't need the approval of a shifter from a rival clan, it was still gratifying to hear praise from someone as strong as Bastian. "Thank you, but I don't think you brought me here to sing my praises."

"No, son, I did not. I am about to share something with you that only the highest ranking members of my pack are privy to, they and the family members of the weres involved."

Bern sat forward in his chair. "Something is wrong." It was a statement not a question.

"Frightfully so. Two of our pups have been kidnapped."

Bern sat back stunned. "How? When?"

"How, we do not know. They were taken from their own beds in the dead of night. No trace, no scent, no tracks. It is as if they vanished into thin air. One was taken last month, the other, two weeks ago. We have increased our night patrols, done everything we can think of, but we have found no trace of the children." Bastian looked at the rug on the floor, his age and the weight of his position showing on his face. Sadness marred his patrician features, and for only a moment he looked defeated. Then determination overcame the weariness. "I will find those children, but I fear I may need help. It is not an easy thing for one such as I to ask for assistance." Bastian locked gazes with Bern. "I ask for an alliance with the Honey Corner's Clan. I will blood bond with you. Stand with you against all enemies, if you will do the same for me."

It was all Bern could do to keep his mouth closed at the unexpected and serendipitous suggestion from the alpha. Bern had a feeling he knew who had stolen the children and they would need all the help they could get protecting both clan and pack if the humans were targeting their progeny.

Bern took a deep breath. "I am deeply honored you would consider such an alliance, Bastian. I will have to discuss it with my clan, but I think the idea has merit. We have had a group of campers under surveillance in the woods outside Honey Corners. We believe they may be HUNTS agents. Do you think it's possible they could have kidnapped your pups?"

Bastian nodded. "I do not know if it was those men, but I do believe it is HUNTS agents who have taken the children. I have heard rumors of this happening in other packs in Tennessee and Louisiana. Not just children, but shifters of all ages disappearing. Also, experiments going on."

"God, why can't they just leave us alone? What have we ever done to them?"

"It's not what we have done, my friend. It's what we are. They want what we have, the freedom from disease, long life, strength. Humans can be greedy, selfish beings," Bastian said with a sad smile.

"You've seen too much in your life haven't you, my friend?"

"Sometimes I fear I have. There is one more thing I must tell you before you bring the prospect of an alliance to your clan. I have enemies."

Bern laughed. "Don't we all?"

"No, you misunderstand me. An Alpha from the north, Sergei, is looking to challenge me. He thinks I am old and weak." Bastian smiled. "He is wrong, of course, but still he is…as you would say, poking the bear." Bastian laughed. "I thought you should be aware of the threat."

Bern nodded. "You are an honorable wolf, Sebastian Von Drake." He downed the balance of his cognac. "Now, let's join our lovely ladies in the moonlight."

"I can think of nothing I would enjoy more." Bastian rose and clapped him on the shoulder. Though their alliance had not yet truly been formed in the formal sense, a bond between the two men had definitely been forged.

The two men stepped onto the moonlit patio and found Jenna, Alice, Martin, Anton and several others sitting in lovely wicker furniture and enjoying the crisp fall evening. Quiet conversation floated to Bern's ears, his sweet Jenna's voice was clear above all the others to him. Telling Alice about her kindergarten class.

Bern stalked up behind her and placed his hands on her shoulders, leaning in to kiss her cheek. "Did you miss me, little one?"

Jenna rubbed her hand through his beard, tangling her fingers in the scruff and pulling him closer. "Always, darling. Isn't it lovely out here tonight? Come sit with us." Bern lifted her from the chair and sat, placing her on his lap, all in one motion. Jenna laughed, nuzzling into his neck and whispering into his ear. "Everything okay?"

Her nodded and whispered back. "Were hearing, remember?"

"No, damn it, I keep forgetting." She giggled. Tucking her face into the crook of his shoulder.

"Get a room, will ya?" Alice groused. "Enough already, with the love feast. We just had dinner for Christ sake."

Bastian stood beside Alice's chair and Bern watched the byplay between the two of them. Bastian was so stiff and formal, he looked down at Alice. "Are you comfortable, Alicia?" he asked.

She looked up, momentarily speechless. "My Daddy used to call me that," she said with a wistful smile. "My parents came to America from Poland when I was seven, he was the only one who called me Alicia."

"I am sorry. Did I bring up a sad memory?" Bastian asked.

Alice smiled sweetly. "No, not at all, a happy memory. I was daddy's girl, I miss him."

"He has passed?" Bastian asked.

"Heart attack, three years ago." Alice shrugged. "I remember him every day. He was the best man I've ever known." She looked down at her lap, hands clasped tightly together.

Jenna reached over and took one of her hands, lacing their fingers, their gazes locked. *Love you*, Jenna mouthed, and Alice smiled.

"We really must be going," Bern said. "Thank you so much for dinner, Bastian." He looked the wolf directly in the eye. "And everything else. I will speak with you soon." He helped Jenna to her feet and stood wrapping his arm around her waist. He extended his other hand to Alice, and the three of them headed into the house and down the hall.

Once the entourage was ensconced in the limousine and on the way back to Honey Corners, Bern opened up about Bastian's revelations.

"Bastian shocked me in more ways than one, my friends," he said, holding Jenna's hand securely in his big paw.

"What's going on, *Sippe*?" Martin asked.

"Two things," Bern said. "I'm sorry, Jenna. I hope you don't mind if we talk business for just a few minutes."

Jenna nodded. "Of course not."

"First, there have been kidnappings in the Von Drake pack. Two cubs have been stolen, right from their beds over the last two months. We need to increase night patrols immediately."

"Oh My God and Goddess," Hans exclaimed from the driver's seat.

Bern nodded, "Yes, I know. It's bad. And the second... The second I think is good, but I need your input, the input of the clan. Sebastian wants to form an alliance. A blood bond between his pack and our clan."

"Are you serious?" Martin shouted. "That hasn't been done in centuries. It is an honor beyond—I can't even think of a word."

"I know. I was half tempted to bond with him on the spot. Especially after feeling his power tonight. That is one powerful werewolf," Bern said.

"What held you back?" Martin asked.

"It is not just me involved," Bern said. "It is the clan, there are advantages, and they are many, but there are disadvantages too. A rival pack is threatening Sebastian. He thinks he will be challenged for power."

"I doubt there is anyone strong enough to defeat him in battle," Hans said.

"I do too," Bern agreed. "But, something is going on, and I have a feeling other things are at play. However, I do think bonding with Sebastian is in our best interest. I just didn't want to make a decision in haste, or without consulting the clan."

"You are good a leader, Bern. A good man. A good bear." Martin clapped him on the shoulder.

Bern's heart swelled with pride, the look in his second's eyes made him feel like a king.

"Call a clan meeting for tomorrow, and make sure the night patrols are increased, starting tonight."

"Done, *Sippe*." Martin pulled out his cell phone and began to make his calls and Bern pulled Jenna onto his lap.

"I suppose I will have to leave you to sleep alone in your bed tonight," he whispered in Jenna's ear.

"No nookie for you, big guy, sorry," she whispered back. Bern kissed her neck. "I guess I will have to settle for a little heavy petting in the backseat," he teased, waggling his eyebrows at her.

Jenna laughed and Alice rolled her eyes. "Oh, give me a break. Can't you two keep your hands off each other for five minutes?"

"Nope," Bern answered with a grin and a kiss to his mate. He loved the blush that covered Jenna's cheeks.

They snuggled together, talking softly and kissing often until too quickly they were pulling into Jenna's driveway. Bern escorted the ladies to the door, did his customary check of the house and sadly left them with only a lingering kiss to his mate on the doorstep.

* * * *

Jenna and Alice were curled up on the opposite ends of the couch, hot chocolate laced with Bailey's warming their hands and their bellies. "Okay, so what's up with you, girl?" Jenna asked.

"What?"

"Don't give me that, you know what I mean. What's the deal with Bastian?"

"No deal. I'm not biting."

"Why not? The man is a hottie."

"He's cute. I'll give you that. In an old world, stuffy, kinda way, but he's not my type."

"Oh, please. If you have a pulse, he's your type. Tall, dark, handsome, powerful, and let's not forget rich as sin. I bet the girls line up for him."

"I'm sure they do, and they can just keep on lining up."

"Come on, Al, you can't tell me you're not at all interested. He's your mate! You have to feel something. I saw it in your eyes."

"Sweetie, I love you. You know that. I wouldn't rain on your parade for anything. I've seen you with Bern and I know you're in love. And it's as plain as the nose on your face that the big bear loves you too. But this mate thing just doesn't work for me. I don't buy the whole thing."

Jenna felt as if Alice had slapped her in the face. A hole opened up in her chest where her heart used to be and tears stung her eyes. "What do you mean, you don't buy it? You were the one that told me to go for it when I met Bern. You said I should grab on with both hands and take my chance at happiness, and now you say you don't buy it."

Alice scooted across the couch and took both Jenna's hands in hers. "Oh, God, don't cry, sweetie. I've made a mess of this. I was right, wasn't I? You and Bern are happy, you're happier than I've ever seen you, but I'm not a love kinda girl." She gave a self-deprecating smile. "I'm not sure I even know how to fall in love, and I'm positive that stuffy old wolf doesn't know what love is. I don't want a, sniff, you're mine. Wham, bam, let's get hitched hook up. It's just not my scene. I'm sorry, Jen, I didn't mean to hurt you. I wouldn't do that for the world, but that man is not for me. I'm carefree, and kinda flighty—"

Jenna interrupted. "Ain't that the truth?"

"Plus, I have my career in Chicago, I'm not going to just drop all I've worked for because of a man. That may sound selfish, but…well, I guess I'm a bit selfish too."

Jenna laughed. "You're really laying out your faults tonight aren't you?"

"I guess I am." Alice laughed. "But, I don't necessarily consider them faults. I am who I am, girl. You know that. I've never pretended otherwise."

"I know, but I don't think Sebastian is going to just give up you know. He's going to pursue you."

"Well, now that might be fun. I'd like to see if I could loosen up the stick in his ass. I don't know how the man manages to walk around with it so far up there." Alice laughed.

"You are terrible!" Jenna sighed.

"Bad to the bone, baby. That's why you love me!"

They fell into each other's arms rolling with laughter.

* * * *

Sunday morning found the biggest bouquet of roses Jenna had ever seen on her doorstep, unfortunately they were not for her. The gorgeous, long stem, red roses were addressed to Miss Alice Miller from none other than Sebastian Von Drake.

Jenna carried the huge bouquet into the kitchen where a half-awake Alice sat sipping coffee. "For you, girl," she said. "I think I'm jealous."

"Damn, that's a lot of freaking flowers."

"No shit. I don't know if I have a vase big enough to put them in. It may take two, or even three!"

Jenna began digging in the cabinets and pulled out several vases, it did indeed take three vases to contain what turned out to be over five dozen roses. "Oh, Alice they are so beautiful!"

Alice put her face to one of the vases and sniffed. "Yes, they are and they smell wonderful." She smiled. "I guess I'll have to call the old bastard and thank him." She laughed.

The doorbell rang and Jenna went to answer, she returned with a huge box of Godiva chocolates, once again for Alice.

"He's pulling out all the stops," Jenna said. "This is enough chocolate to cure my PMS for a year." She laughed.

"Ha, you are so easy, that wouldn't even last me the month," Alice said. "But it's a good start. Crack that baby open, let's have a taste."

"It's nine o'clock in the morning!"

"It's never too early for chocolate."

"Oh, well that's true." Jenna opened the box and they both stood drooling over the contents for several moments before they could stir themselves to make a choice. "Oh my God, how do I pick just one? It's almost a shame to eat them, they're so beautiful."

"Beautiful, smootiful, taste is all that counts, lemme at em." Alice took a piece and popped it in her mouth, her eyes closed and she rolled her head back. "Oh my God, it's almost better than sex."

"I wouldn't go that far," Jenna said.

"I said, almost." Alice laughed. "Now, I really have to call the old goat, I mean wolf. I suppose Bern has his number, right?"

"Yes, I'm sure he does. I was just about to call him anyway."

"Oh, I'm sure." She glanced at her watch. "It's been almost eight hours since you talked to him, you must be in withdrawals by now."

Jenna threw a chocolate at her. "You are such a snarky bitch."

Alice caught the chocolate and popped it in her mouth. "That's why you love me." She stood up and kissed Jenna on the head. "I'll give you some privacy." She turned to leave the room. "Don't forget to get the old bastard's number for me...and give Bern a kiss for me." She blew Jenna an air kiss as she ducked out of the room.

Jenna grabbed her cell and dialed Bern, he picked up on the first ring. "Hello, beautiful."

"Hi, Bern. I miss you."

"I miss you too. I especially missed you in my bed last night."

Jenna felt her cheeks warm. "How are things this morning? Did Martin get the clan meeting set up?"

"Yes, everything is all set. I wanted to talk to you about that. I'd like you to come."

"To the clan meeting?"

"Yes."

"But, I'm not part of the clan."

"Yes, you are, little one. You are the mate of the clan leader. I'd like to introduce you to the clan."

Jenna twisted a strand of hair around the finger of her free hand, she was always nervous about meeting new people, she was never comfortable in crowds, had always been the wallflower. She was the fat girl in the corner, was she going to embarrass Bern?

"What are you thinking, little one? I can feel your anxiety."

"I don't know if I like your being able to sense my feelings. I don't want to embarrass you. I'm…"

"You are beautiful, smart, precious, and mine. Trust me, little one, they will love you as much as I do."

Tears pricked Jenna's eyes. "Oh, Bern, I love you so much."

"I wish I was there to hold you in my arms. Will you come over? I can send a car for you."

"Sure, in about an hour? I need to shower and get dressed. Do you have Sebastian's phone number?"

"Yes, why would you need Sebastian's number?"

"He sent Alice flowers and chocolates this morning, she wants to call and thank him. He showed you up by the way."

"Oh really? How so?"

"He sent Alice over five dozen red roses, I'm jealous."

"I'm sorry, little one. I have been remiss in my courtly duties. I shall have to remedy that in the future."

Jenna laughed. "It doesn't count you know, if I have to ask."

"Oh, I will surprise you when you least expect it."

"We'll see," she said. "I better run, if I'm going to be ready when your car gets here."

"Okay, I will see you soon, little one."

Chapter Eleven

Jenna dressed carefully, she didn't want to be overdressed, but she wanted to look nice to meet Bern's clan. She chose her favorite multicolored patchwork skirt and paired it with a three-quarter length sleeved cream colored blouse and hand-crocheted burgundy vest.

She left her hair down and curled around her shoulders, as that was the way Bern appeared to like it best. She was applying the last touches to her make-up when the doorbell rang. Tossing the mascara back into her purse, she jogged to the door.

"I'm heading out," she called to Alice.

"Kiss the bear for me," she replied. "I've got plenty of work to keep me busy."

"Okay, there are frozen meals in the 'fridge."

"Gotcha. Have fun!"

"Love ya. Bye."

Hans waited on the doorstep. "Hi, Hans. How are you?"

"I am well, Miss Raynes."

"How many times do I have to tell you to call me Jenna?"

Hans blushed. "Jenna." She grabbed his arm and walked toward the car. "Let's go." Jenna refused to sit in the back and sat herself in the front seat next to Hans. "I don't know if Bern would approve Miss…"

"Shut it, Hans. Bern won't mind my sitting in the front seat. I would feel stupid sitting in the back seat all by myself. This way we can talk."

Hans walked around to the driver's side, slid inside the car and turned over the engine. He cleared his throat. "Alice is not joining us?"

"No." Jenna laughed. "She's working. So, what time is the clan meeting?"

"Four o'clock, ma'am."

"Ma'am? Really? Hans, that's not any better than Miss Raynes, is Jenna so hard to say? Try it now. Jenna, J e n n a. You can do it."

Jenna was trying very hard not to laugh, but Hans' face was turning a peculiar shade of purple.

"Jenna," he mumbled.

"See! I knew you could do it! From now on if you don't call me Jenna I'm going to flick you on the nose. Don't think I won't," she said waving her finger in the direction of his face.

She couldn't hold the laughter in any longer and burst out a loud guffaw. Hans gave her a stern look and then joined in the laughter. "Okay, I give, Jenna. I think you will be good for Bern and our clan."

Jenna reached across the car and took his hand. "Hans, I love Bern. I don't know you that well, or most of your clan, but I want only the best for you all."

Hans was stopped at a stoplight and he looked deeply into her eyes. "I can see that, Jenna." He squeezed her hand and turned his attention back to the road.

"Do you have a mate, Hans?"

"I think I have met my mate, but it's complicated."

"I'm sorry. Doesn't she return your affections?"

Hans laughed. "Um, it isn't a lady. Ladies aren't, um, my preference," he mumbled.

It was Jenna's turn to blush. "I'm sorry, Hans, I shouldn't have made an assumption."

Hans smiled self-deprecatingly. "It's all right, most people assume, because of my size and position that I'm straight. I don't take offense."

Jenna patted his hand. "Well, I shouldn't have assumed, and I'm sorry. Is there a stigma in the were community about being gay, like there is in the human world?"

"Surprisingly, not as much. I guess we have so much other prejudice, we don't look for more reasons to hate."

Jenna ran a hand down Hans' cheek. "So, what is the problem with your mate?"

"He is of a higher rank then me, and not of our clan. He didn't even acknowledge me when we met. I don't know what to do." Hans looked crestfallen.

"Maybe you should approach him," Jenna said.

"That wouldn't be appropriate."

"More of this political crap, right?"

Hans looked uncomfortable. "Yes, I'm afraid so."

"I'm sick of politics. You want me to talk to him?"

"That is very sweet of you, m…Jenna, but no, thank you."

"I will, you know. I'll kick his bear ass. Well, that didn't come out quite right."

Hans laughed. "He's not a bear," he mumbled. "You are very sweet, Jenna, and thank you again, but it wouldn't be…"

"Appropriate," she finished. "Yeah, I get it. If you ever need to talk I'm here, Hans. I mean it."

He reached across and squeezed her hand. "Thank you, Jenna. I see the look of peace on Bern's face when he holds your hand… something I haven't seen since his parents died. I long for a mate to soothe my soul." A dreamy, wistful look crossed Hans' face and the realization struck Jenna that mating was more than just the coming together of two people to the were community. It was something sacred.

They pulled into the driveway of Bern's house and he was in the open doorway before the car had come to a complete stop. Han's jumped out and came around to her side to let her out. She and Bern met halfway up the walkway, just like a scene in one of those romantic commercials, he rushed toward her as she rushed toward him, all that was missing was the field of flowers.

He picked her up, spinning her in a circle as he devoured her lips in a burning kiss. "God I missed you, little one," he mumbled against her lips.

"It was only one night." She laughed.

"One night too long. I can't stand to be away from you." He set her on her feet, keeping his arm securely around her and led her into the house. "Is Alice settled?"

"Yes, thanks. After much yelling on the phone, which I assume was with Bastian. She informed me, she'd had enough of shifters for the day. She's working, as usual, from her laptop at my house. Hans said the clan isn't coming until four?"

"That's right, but Sebastian is coming at two."

"Really? You're going to bond today then?"

"Yes. It's been decided, and we need to go over all the details with our inner circles." He looked at his watch. "Which gives me three hours to enjoy with my mate before business takes precedence."

He scooped her up in his arms. "So, where shall I take my sweet morsel?" He nuzzled her neck. "My office? I haven't ravished you there yet."

"No!" Jenna shrieked. "Someone could come in."

"Not unless they have a death wish," Bern growled. "The bedroom then?" Jenna nodded against his shoulder. "Mmm, sounds good to me, more room to play," he growled. Bern threw her over his shoulder in a fireman's carry and took the stairs two at a time until he reached the bedroom. He slammed the door shut with his foot and placed Jenna on her feet in front of a low dresser with a mirror attached. He turned her to face the mirror.

"Look at this, a present for me to unwrap," he said as he placed his hands on her shoulders and slowly slid the vest from her arms. He tossed the vest toward the chair in the corner of the room. He pulled the blouse from the waist band of her skirt and skimmed it up and over her head, Jenna lifted her arms to assist him.

She watched her image in the mirror, flushed with arousal, she was naked from the waist up, save for her beige lace push-up bra. Bern tucked his thumbs into the elastic waistband of her skirt and eased it to the floor, following it down until he was on his knees. "Lift," he said, tapping one foot and then the other. "Oh, I like these boots," he said, indicating her knee high brown suede three-inch heels. "I think I'll leave them on."

He licked the skin above the top of her boots, the back of her knees and up the back of her thighs. Bern slid his hands up the front of her legs, letting them rest at the top of her thighs, teasing the crease where her thigh met her mons. He lightly bit one juicy butt cheek, eliciting a squeal from Jenna, then licked away the sting.

Bern kissed the dimples at the base of her spine and twirled his tongue in the small depressions. "Put your hands on the dresser and spread your legs," he instructed. Jenna shivered as she complied. Bern traced the seam between her rear cheeks down to her sex, he licked from her clit all the way back, spreading her cheeks and tickling her rosette with his tongue. "I'll take you here one day, little one."

Jenna gasped.

"Nothing to say to that, little one? Does that thought frighten you? Excite you?"

"Both?" Jenna squeaked.

Bern slapped her cheek. "Good answer." He licked her sex again. She could feel her cream flooding her channel. Bern dipped a finger inside and tickled her clit with his tongue, Jenna could feel her orgasm climbing closer.

Bern shifted positions, moving his hands to the front of her body, he kept one hand teasing her clit and moved the other to fondle her breast, he kissed and licked his way up her spine, until he reached the mating mark on her neck.

"My bear is riding me hard, little one. He wants to mark you again, wants his scent and mark clear for all to note."

"Yes, do it. I need you."

Bern pulled her hips toward him and entered her in one swift thrust. Jenna cried out in pleasure, grinding back against him. Bern's arms surrounded her, holding her hips as he pounded into her. Jenna grasped the edge of the dresser and held on for dear life. Her breasts bounced madly, and watching the scene was the hottest thing she had ever seen.

She could tell Bern was nearing his peak, his thrusts were becoming erratic. "Bern, I need..."

He growled and his fangs elongated, he struck in exactly the same place as before, re-piercing her mating mark, and Jenna came with a scream she was sure the entire household heard. Two more thrusts and Bern followed her, only his arms around her kept her from collapsing in a heap to the floor. She didn't faint this time, but she was damn close. Bern withdrew from her and lifted her in his arms, carrying her to the bed, placing her in the center and crawling in to spoon up beside her.

He held her tightly, her back to his front, while she floated back to earth. He stroked her hair and kissed her temple and cheek, the only places he could reach in that position. When her breathing finally returned to normal she turned her head and caught his lips in a sweet kiss. "I love you," she whispered.

"I love you too, little one."

"I think I need a nap."

Bern chuckled. "Sleep, my sweet. I will hold you while you dream."

Jenna closed her eyes and was asleep before her next breath.

She awakened to someone gently kissing her neck. "Mmm, that's nice."

"It's time to wake up, Sleeping Beauty."

Jenna rolled to her back and stretched. "What time is it?"

"One-thirty."

"One-thirty! Crap, I need to take a shower and fix my make-up!"

"No shower. My bear wants his scent on you."

"Seriously? You want me to go out there and meet all those people smelling like sex?"

"I most certainly do."

Jenna sat up in bed and gave him the evil eye. Bern would not back down. "I'm guessing this is a bear thing?"

"A were thing, you could say."

"All right. I don't like it, but for you I'll do it, but I'm at least washing up."

Bern laughed. "Yes, my little one. You know where the bathroom is."

"Where is my purse?"

"I think you dropped it somewhere downstairs."

As Jenna scurried for the bathroom, she shouted over her shoulder. "Well, will you please go down and get it? I need my makeup."

"I don't think you need makeup, you are beautiful without it."

"Bern, I'm not going to argue with you. Go get my purse or I'm going to do to you what I told Hans I was going to do to him and flick you on the nose."

Bern laughed. "Oh my God, I would have loved to have seen Hans' face when you told him that. What did he say?"

"He agreed. He did turn a pretty shade of purple though."

"Agreed to what?"

"To stop calling me Miss Raynes, or ma'am and call me Jenna."

"Oh, that will be hard for the clan members, little one. There is a lot of formality in clan business."

"I get that, that's why I'm starting now. My momma always said 'start the way you intend to continue.'"

"Your mom sounds like a smart lady."

"She is, I can't wait for you to meet her."

"I'm looking forward to it. When are you going to tell them about us?"

"I was going to tell them today. Maybe we can call them tonight, when things calm down?"

"That sounds like a plan."

"God, I'm so nervous. What if your clan doesn't like me?"

"I've already told you, they will love you. Besides, you've already won over the toughest members, Martin, Guiles, Hans and Julia."

"Julia is tough?"

"Are you kidding? She is terrible! No one has ever been good enough for me up until now, yet she sings your praises like you are Mother Teresa."

"I wouldn't go that far."

"You haven't heard her when you're not around."

Jenna came out of the bathroom, running her fingers through her hair. "Really? That's so nice. I like her a lot too. Sarah is the cutest thing! And little Jimmy is adorable too, I can't wait to meet all your nieces and nephews."

Bern stepped close and pulled her into his arms. "I can't wait to start making a few babies of our own." Jenna rubbed her face on his still naked chest and looked up into his eyes. "Really?"

"Yeah, really."

They kissed sweetly and then she pulled back. "Where's my purse?"

Bern sighed. "Hans should be here with it in a minute."

"You better get dressed," she worried.

"Hans has seen me naked before."

Jenna tsked at him, and he turned to the closet to pull on some slacks and a shirt, just as a knock sounded at the door.

"Thank you, Hans," Jenna said taking the bag from his hands. "We'll be down in a minute."

"Yes, ma'am," Hans said with a nod. She lifted an eyebrow at him. "I mean Jenna."

She nodded. "Okay, see you soon." She closed the door and crossed to the bathroom mirror, leaving the door open, she dumped the contents of her purse on the vanity and rummaged for her foundation.

Jenna quickly applied foundation, blush, powder, eye shadow, mascara and lipstick, while she heard Bern grumbling in the bedroom about females and taking forever to get ready.

She shoved everything back in her purse and stepped back into the bedroom with the clutch under her arm, swinging her hair around her shoulders. "Ready to go."

Bern stood up from the bed and came over to kiss her. "Worth the wait too. I guess."

"Don't muss my lipstick."

"Oh, that will not work," he said, taking his finger and rubbing the lipstick from her lips, he kissed her soundly. "You can wear lip gloss, because I will kiss you anytime I want, little one."

"Bossy bear," she muttered and she dug a lip gloss from her bag and swiped her lips.

"Mmm, strawberry," Bern hummed. "Better yet."

"You're terrible!"

"And you love it."

She smacked his arm. "It's a good thing I love you or I would have to put you in your place."

He kissed her nose. "Yep, good thing." He took her arm and led her from the room. "Let's wait in my office. Sebastian should be here soon."

Jenna looked at her watch, it was 1:53, and yeah Sebastian would be here soon. When they reached the bottom of the stairs they could hear a car pulling into the driveway, so they bypassed the office and headed to the front door.

Jenna and Bern stood side by side outside the open front door waiting for Sebastian and his entourage to exit his SUV.

The driver exited first, surveying the area from behind his dark mirrored glasses before he moved around to the passenger side and opened the door for Sebastian's second, Anton. Anton carefully scented the air, walked a full circle around the vehicle and then returned to open the back seat door of the SUV. Victor and two other men Jenna didn't recognize left the vehicle, forming a tunnel into which Sebastian exited.

He stepped forward, surrounded by his men and they walked forward as a group toward the front porch. Once they reached the steps, Bastian waved a hand to halt the men's progress and walked forward with his hand extended to Bern. The two men shook and then Bastian leaned in to kiss Jenna's cheek.

"It's so good to see you again, my friends."

"You as well, my friend," Bern said, clapping him on the shoulder. "Let's go to my office."

"Come along, men," he called over his shoulder.

It was a good thing Bern had a spacious office because seven very large shifters and one not so small soon to be shifted lady took up a lot of room. The men scattered around the office and settled on couches and chairs, Bern distributed drinks and then took the place of power behind the huge oak desk with Jenna perched on his lap.

How a mood could be somber and joyous at the same time, Jenna didn't quite understand, but that was the feeling in the room. The men were happy, yet you could tell the event was a momentous occasion.

Sebastian was the first to speak, he leaned forward in his chair. "Bern, gentlemen, I am pleased and honored to be here today. I hope this is but the first of many gatherings between our circles."

Bern tightened his grip on Jenna. "Bastian, you do me a great honor by bonding with me today. I am aware of your power. I feel it in my bones. I believe our union will be beneficial to all concerned, and I pray to God and Goddess that all shifters remain safe from harm."

All the members of the group voiced words of agreement, from "Amens." To "I'll second that."

Bern tapped Jenna on the hip and she stood, he walked around the desk until he was standing in front of Sebastian. "We will conduct the ritual in the circle at sunset, before my clan tonight, and then again tomorrow in front of your pack. Is this acceptable to you, Alpha Von Drake?"

Sebastian stood, and the two men were eye to eye. They clasped arms, hand to wrist, in a warrior's handshake. "It is acceptable, *Sippe* Helms," he responded with a nod of his head, and with that the formality was ended. Bastian's face broke into a broad grin and he slapped Bern on the shoulder.

"Now, lead me to this famous bar-b-que I've heard so much about!" he said.

"I've got a whole pig in the pit roasting away," Bern said. "It's gonna be good eats tonight."

"Oh, man. That sounds great," said Viktor. "I love roast pig."

"Let's head out to the patio, beer's in the coolers," said Martin. "The clan members will be arriving soon and we can start making introductions. We're expecting about two hundred to show up tonight, because the *Sippe* is introducing his mate. This is going to be one hell of a clan meeting."

Martin hadn't been exaggerating. People kept arriving, one after the other and every one brought some kind of dish to the pot luck gathering. Jenna had never seen so much food in her life. So far there were six banquet tables covered with casserole dishes, salad bowls, cheese trays and every kind of dessert you could think of. Jenna was thinking of stealing a peanut butter pie and hiding out in the kitchen, no one would miss one little pie, right?

Jenna had always been a nervous eater and meeting all these people and being the center of attention was definitely making her nervous. Arms reached around from behind her and gave her a hug from behind. Jenna jumped a foot.

"I'm sorry, darlin', I didn't mean to scare you," Julia said.

"It's okay, I'm just kind of jumpy. I'm glad to see a familiar face." She turned to Julia with a smile. "Are the kids here?"

"No, James' mother is babysitting, children aren't really welcome at clan meetings. Those that aren't coming take turns watching the kids for the ones that are coming."

"Oh." Jenna could feel her face fall, she was hoping for some little ones to keep her distracted. She looked over the crowd behind Julia. "Where is James?"

Julia shrugged. "He's around here somewhere. He probably found Bern and his cronies and is shooting the bull. So, are you excited about the introduction ceremony?"

Jenna squirmed. "Um, yeah sure."

Julia arched an eyebrow at her. "That has the crackle of Confederate money. What's the matter?"

"I hate being the center of attention. I'm afraid I'll embarrass Bern. I'm not beautiful or sophisticated, or…" She shrugged.

Julia hugged her, and then held her by the shoulders and looked into her eyes. "Jenna, you have to understand something about shifters. Humans place a lot of emphasis on outward things—physical appearance, status, sophistication. For shifters, it's all about what's inside—strength, power, heart, soul. Something in your soul touched Bern's. That's all the clan will care about. Plus I've seen your heart. I see how you are with the children, Sarah adores you. I can already tell you and I will be the best of friends. Just relax, Jenna, you are already one of us."

The sincerity in her eyes was hard to ignore and Jenna felt some of the tension in her shoulders loosen. "Thank you. I think we'll be good friends too." She leaned in and kissed Julia's cheek.

"Now, did you see that dessert table? I think we should steal a pie and sneak off to the kitchen," Julia said.

Jenna laughed. "That's what I was thinking when you walked up!"

"Peanut butter!" they said together and laughed like loons. Bern walked up and laid his hands on Jenna's shoulders. "What's so funny?" Both women laughed harder and almost fell over in their mirth.

Bern looked between Jenna and his sister and shook his head. James had joined them and looked at his brother-in-law. "Do you have any idea what's going on, James?"

"Not a clue, but I've learned not to ask," James answered.

Julia wrapped her arms around her husband and kissed his cheek. "Good answer, husband." Julia finally managed to control her laughter enough to speak.

Jenna threw an arm around Bern's waist and leaned against him. "Julia was just trying to make me less nervous," she said.

"Well, it looks like she succeeded," Bern said.

"Yes, she did," Jenna responded with a smile. "She is an angel."

"Oh my God, stand back, James, lightning is gonna strike."

Julia punched him in the arm. "I am so unappreciated! It's a good thing I have a new sister, because my brother is a brat."

"Your sisters would say the same thing." Bern chuckled.

Julia blew a raspberry at him.

"So mature, Jules," Bern said with a wink at Jenna.

"Stop being mean to my sister." She nudged him with an elbow.

"You're taking her side?" Bern asked.

"Of course! We girls have to stick together," Jenna replied.

"Great," James muttered. "As if we weren't already outnumbered enough."

"We'll just have to have lots of sons, so we can even out the group," Bern said with a nod.

Jenna could feel the blush crawl across her face to the roots of her hair. She looked at him in shock.

"Just for that, I think I'll only have girls!"

"You know it's the man's sperm that determines the sex of the child?" Bern intoned sagely.

"And you know I can close my legs and say this station is closed for business, right?" Jenna snipped.

Julia grabbed James' arm and said. "I think we better be going now, you started a shit storm, and I don't want to be here for the fall out."

The two bears skulked away while Jenna glared at Bern.

Bern advanced slowly toward Jenna and put his hands on her shoulders, she shrugged them off and turned her back. He wrapped his arms around her from behind and started kissing her neck. She tried to stay mad, but damn, that felt so good, involuntarily her head tipped to the side to give him better access.

"Are we seriously fighting about whether we will have boys or girls as children?"

Jenna felt another blush, this one from embarrassment instead of anger. She turned in his arms. "I'm sorry, I can't believe I flew off the handle like that. I'm just so nervous, I over-reacted."

"I'm sorry too. I shouldn't be teasing you when I know you're all keyed up." He kissed her tenderly on the lips, brushing his tongue across the seam, seeking entrance. She opened for him and their tongues mated, reaffirming their bond with passion and caring.

Chapter Twelve

"Goddess be with you." Bern intoned from the center of the circle. Jenna stood to his right and Sebastian to his left. Martin, Guiles and Hans stood behind Bern. Anton, Viktor and Ivan stood behind Sebastian.

The meeting had begun. "Brotherhood, strength and honor hold the circle," the assembled group replied and Jenna felt goose bumps cover her skin.

"It is my honor and privilege tonight to not only present to the clan my beloved mate, but also to join in a blood bond with my brother wolf, Sebastian Von Drake."

Gasps and murmurs rippled through the crowd and Bern raised his hands to silence them. "I know this comes as a surprise to some of you, and frankly the offer came as a surprise to me. A blood bond has not been formed in centuries and we are honored to be joining with the Von Drake Pack."

Cheers went up from the crowd. Bern turned to Sebastian with a nod and the two men stepped forward and faced one another. They stood with their hands on each other's shoulders.

Sebastian spoke in a voice that rippled with power. "I, Sebastian Von Drake pledge my loyalty, my fealty, my strength, my honor, my sword, my claws, my wisdom and my brotherhood to Bern Helms and the Honey Corners Clan from this day until death takes my soul."

Jenna shivered as the power spread throughout the glen. Bern's voice boomed with more power than she'd ever heard from him in the past. "I, Bern Helms pledge my fealty, my strength, my honor, my sword, my claws, my wisdom, and my brotherhood to Sebastian Von Drake and the Von Drake Pack from this day until death takes my soul."

Both men struck at once, turning their heads and biting into the wrist of the right hand resting on their shoulder. Though the night was clear, lightning lit the sky. The men released the bites, blood dripped from the wounds and fell to the ground, the two men threw back their heads and a roar came from Bern's throat, while Bastian howled like the wolf he was.

Echoing sounds came from the crowd, along with cheers and whoops of joy. Bern and Bastian licked their wounds to stop the bleeding, and then leaned forward and embraced in a man hug. Thumping each other's backs and then pulling back to stare into each other's eyes.

Jenna could feel the connection between them from her spot five feet away. It was almost scary.

She couldn't wait to talk to Bern about it. With their arms clasped around each other's shoulders they turned to face the clan as one. Each raising their free outside hand to call for quiet. The crowd settled and the two men nodded.

"We two are now one," Bern said. "One heart, one spirit, one clan."

"One pack," Sebastian added.

More cheering rose from the group. Again the men signaled for quiet, this time Sebastian spoke. "I believe we have a joyous event to celebrate this evening, and if Bern would allow me. I would like to be the first to introduce you all to your *Sippe's* new mate." Bern nodded, Sebastian stepped away and extended a hand toward Jenna.

Her hands were shaking, but she put her trembling hand in his and he placed it in Bern's large paw.

"I present to you, Jenna Marie Raynes, *Sippe* Mate, and..." he looked deep into her eyes, that power and strength he wore so well filling her soul, "...extraordinary person. May she bring *our* clan the peace and joy that she has brought our leader."

Bern enfolded her in his arms and kissed her sweetly. The cheers of the crowd faded away and all that remained was her big bear, holding her tightly in his embrace. The kiss was a promise of things to come, not of the passion they had already shared, though she was sure there would be much more passion to share in the future, but of a lifetime together.

When he finally lifted his head, tears shimmered in her eyes and he surreptitiously wiped them away. "I love you, little one," he leaned in and whispered.

"I love you too," she tearfully responded.

Bern put his arm behind her back and turned to the clan. "My Mate! My Jenna!" he shouted.

The cheers and shouting that ensued could probably be heard in Nashville. Jenna wondered if her parents could hear them sitting out on their front porch and stifled a giggle at the thought. When everyone had finally calmed down, Bern called an end to the meeting with more of the formality and pomp, and then everyone descended on the food like a pack of dogs on a three-legged cat.

While everyone was scattering Sebastian pulled Jenna to the side. "Where is the lovely Alice this evening?"

"I'm sorry, Bastian. She stayed at my house to work. She got your flowers and chocolates, she said she was going to call you. Didn't she?"

"Yes, she called," he said with a deflated look. "She thanked me, but declined my invitation to meet for dinner. Why is she so against seeing me again? It can't really be just her career."

"I'm sorry, Bastian, but that's not my story to tell. Alice is a wonderful woman, she has a heart of gold and if she loves you, she would do anything for you. But she surrounds herself in a suit of armor and very few break through. If you are one of the lucky ones, you'll have the best girl in the world. I wish you luck." Jenna leaned up and kissed his cheek.

"Are you pulling for me, or are you against me?" he asked, with a quirked brow.

She raised a brow right back at him. "That remains to be seen. I am pulling for Alice. If I see that you are right for her…We'll just have to wait and see." With that she turned to go and find her mate.

She found him sitting at one of the many picnic tables with his sister Julia and James and several others she didn't recognize. Coming up behind him and placing a hand on his shoulder, he reached up to pull her onto his lap.

"Hello, love," he said. "Meet a few more of the crew, these are my sisters, Andrea and Dagmar and their husbands, Artie and Kevin."

"Hi, I didn't know more of Bern's family would be here tonight. It's nice to meet you. I can't wait until dinner Wednesday when we can all get together and really talk," Jenna said.

"Me either," replied Andrea. "What about your family, when will we get to meet them?"

Jenna felt her cheek heat. "I'm not sure yet. My parents are supposed to be coming up for Christmas. We haven't had a chance to tell them yet, with everything going on. We were actually going to call them tonight and give them the good news," Jenna said with a smile.

"Oh," Dagmar said frowning. "Do you think they will be okay with it? Do they have a problem with shifters?"

Jenna shook her head adamantly. "No, not at all. My parents are very open minded. They were very supportive of me when I got the job here. The only thing they didn't like was that it was so far away from them. They have no problems with shifters."

"Yeah, well, it's one thing to say it and something else to be faced with your daughter being mated to one," Dagmar muttered.

Anger started burning in Jenna's gut, who did this sow think she was to judge her parent's? She's never even met them for Christ's sake. "Easy, little one," Bern whispered in her ear. "Kevin was human and his parent's didn't take their mating very well. Dagmar is a tad bitter. Don't take it personally."

"How can I not take it personally, she's attacking my parents and she doesn't even know them. And I told you to quit doing that. I don't like you in my head!"

Bern laughed and nuzzled her neck. "Can't help it, little one. I'm in there, I just feel your emotions, especially when they are that strong. Please don't strangle my sister. I know I have five, but the others would miss her."

That diffused Jenna's anger and she laughed. "Okay, I'll let her live…for now."

"And by the way, you called her a sow," he teased.

"Oh my God, I did, you heard that?" Jenna covered her mouth with her hands and then laughed hysterically. Everyone at the table looked at her like she'd grown two heads, which just made her laugh harder.

When she finally got herself under control her head was laying on Bern's shoulder and he was holding her trembling body, to keep her from falling on the ground. "Sorry." She hiccupped.

"Wanna let us in on the joke?" Julia asked. "I could use a good laugh."

Bern shook his head. "Um, no. Private joke."

Thank God, Sebastian and his entourage chose that moment to walk up. Bern placed Jenna on her feet and stood.

"Bern, we had a lovely evening. We're going to take our leave now."

"Thank you so much, Sebastian. We'll see you out." Bern nodded to his family and turned to escort his guests to the front door with a hand on the small of Jenna's back.

Sebastian's SUV idled outside the ornate front doors, one of his minions obviously having retrieved the vehicle. His guards surrounded them on the porch and Jenna, Bern and Sebastian shared a private moment.

Sebastian first looked at Jenna. "You, my dear, are a lovely lady, and will make a fine *Sippe's* mate. Thank you for allowing me to be a part of your ceremony." He kissed both of her cheeks, and for once Bern didn't growl.

He then turned to Bern, the look they exchanged was long and full of hidden meaning. Jenna could only wonder what they shared through their connection. "Good night, my brother," he said as he embraced Bern.

"Good night, my brother," Bern returned.

Jenna would swear both men's eyes were suspiciously damp when they pulled apart, though she was certain they would both deny it.

* * * *

Everyone finally left, and the house was quiet. Jenna and Bern sat in the living room snuggled on the couch before a low crackling fire, sipping hot chocolate and relaxing from the stress of the day.

Bern toyed with a curl of hair on her temple. "Are you ready to call your folks?" he asked.

Jenna snuggled closer and released a soft sigh. "Yes, I guess."

"You're not nervous, are you?"

"No, not really. Excited, kind of nervous. I know Mom and Dad are going to love you. Where's my purse?" She lifted her head to look around.

Bern pulled his cell from his hip holster. "My phone is right here, just use it. Then I'll have their number programed in," he said with a smile.

"That works." Jenna took the phone and dialed.

Her mother answered on the second ring. "Rayne residence. How can I help you?" The unfamiliar number putting her into her professional mode.

"Hi, Mom, it's Jenna."

"Jenna! Where are you calling from? Is everything all right?"

"Calm down, Mother. Everything is fine. I'm calling from my...um, fiancé's phone."

"Fiancé! Did you say...? Barton! Get your fanny down here, your daughter just said she has a fiancé!"

Her father picked up the other extension. "Baby girl, is that you?"

"No, Daddy, it's your other daughter. Of course it's me. How are you?"

"Fit as a fiddle. What's this I hear about a fiancé?"

"I'm engaged! His name is Bern Helms, he's right here, he'd like to speak to you."

Jenna handed Bern the phone. "Hello, Mr. and Mrs. Raynes. It's a pleasure to meet you. I wish we could have met in person, but that will come soon enough. I love your daughter very much, we are already mated and will marry when arrangements can be made."

"Mated?" Barton said. "So I take it you are a shifter?"

"Yes, sir. I am a grizzly shifter. Alpha of my clan."

"Good, then you will never hurt my daughter."

Bern held the phone out and looked at it, of all the responses he had run through in his mind, that one hadn't even entered the picture.

"No, sir. I would never hurt my Jenna. I would die to keep her safe."

Barton laughed. "You misunderstand me, son. You think like a shifter. I know you will keep her physically safe, but I meant you would never hurt her emotionally. Never cheat on her, mess around, like these stupid young punks now-a-days that you can't trust as far as you can throw them."

Cassandra broke in. "Oh, I can't wait to meet you, Bern. We were planning to come down for Christmas, but maybe we will move it up and come for Thanksgiving. What do you think? Barton, could you get away then?"

"We'll see, Kiki. Where's my daughter, is she listening in?"

"I'm here, Daddy," Jenna said, Bern held the phone so they could both hear.

"I'm so happy for you baby. If your mother has her way, and you know she will, we'll be there in November, but we'll talk to you next Sunday."

"We love you," they both said.

"I love you too," Jenna said, and they both hung up. Bern hooked the phone back into the holster on his belt and Jenna laid her head on his shoulder. "That went well."

"Yes, it did. Your father sure didn't seem to care that you mated a shifter."

"I told you he wouldn't."

"I know you did, but I have to say I had my reservations."

Jenna sat up and looked into his eyes, in them she saw reflected the pain of years of prejudice. She leaned in and tenderly kissed his lips, palming his cheeks and then running her fingers through his shaggy brown hair.

For long minutes they gently caressed and kissed, passion took a backseat to warmth and affection. Jenna's hands travelled over Bern's muscled back, moving constantly, mapping the hills and valleys of the sculpted terrain.

Bern's hands tangled in Jenna's curls, holding her head in place for his kisses. When they finally broke apart, he leaned his forehead against hers and breathed deep of her scent. "I love you, my mate."

"I love you too, my big bear," she said. They rested like that for a moment, and then she stirred. "I hate to say it, but I better go home. Alice is waiting, and tomorrow is a school day."

Bern kissed her nose. "You're right, little one. I will take you home."

* * * *

In the dark of night the HUNTS crew planned their mission. No fire burned at the campsite tonight. The men were all dressed in black, camouflage on their faces. They gathered in a circle around a map with a flashlight.

"Okay, the damn wolf warned the fucking bears and they've increased the night patrols, but I still think we can make the grab tonight. The Schmidt's house is at the edge of town, and we have enough sleeping gas for two rooms. If we time the grab between the roving patrols, and take out one of the guards with a tranquilizer dart, if necessary, we can grab the Schmidt kid before midnight."

"I want to hit the bears fast and get out of town. While they are out searching for the Schmidt kid, we'll hit the playground after school tomorrow afternoon and get Sarah Barr, then we'll take both kids to the lab," John said.

"That means we have to keep Jacob Schmidt here until tomorrow afternoon, aren't you afraid the bears will find him?" Scott asked.

"We won't keep him here," John said. "We'll keep him sedated and in the van. It will only be eighteen hours, I have enough scent blocker to keep him hidden for that long and we can keep the van moving."

"Maybe we should wait and snatch the kid closer to morning," Kyle said. "Hit the house like four am, then we wouldn't have to hold the kid so long, or be on the run as long."

John scratched the scruff on his chin. "That's a thought. Good thinking Kyle. It also gives us a chance to get a little sleep tonight. Okay men, set your alarms for three and hit the rack." He slapped Kyle on the shoulder and the men dispersed.

John went over to check the equipment in the van, Kyle followed. "Everything set?" Kyle asked.

"Yeah, I've got sleeping gas for two rooms, twelve tranquillizer darts and twenty scent blocker pills," John replied.

"Are you sure this tranquillizer is strong enough for bears?"

John quirked a brow at him. "Yes, I'm sure."

Kyle raised his hands in a defensive gesture. "Just checking."

"Get some sleep, I don't want any mistakes tonight."

Kyle saluted. "Yes, sir." He turned and headed to his tent.

At three o'clock the men gathered and took their scent blocker pills, the pills worked within thirty minutes, so by the time they reached the outskirts of town they would have no scent.

"Move out," John said and the men piled into three vehicles, the van and two jeeps. They drove to the edge of town and parked the jeeps in the woods, concealing the vehicles. They drove the van as close to the house as possible, still keeping out of sight.

According to their reconnaissance, the guards shouldn't be due to patrol this area until five am so they had an hour to get in and out. John grabbed the tanks of sleeping gas, it was a formula the scientists had come up with of aerosolized Ketamine, Rohypnol and God only knew what else, John sure didn't want to know. But it worked great for their purposes. The animal tranquilizer put the weres to sleep and Rohypnol made them forget anything they might have heard of the crew during the kidnapping.

The couple would wake in the morning, astonished to find their child missing. Saying they had never heard or seen a thing. It was beautiful.

The fall weather made things even easier, the windows were open to the cool night air, so all John had to do was slip the hose through the open window and open the valve. Ten minutes and the drug had taken effect.

He moved to the child's window and repeated the process. The men donned gas masks and entered through the open window. John injected the child with a dose of Ketamine to make sure he stayed asleep and carried him out to the van.

Metal cages were built into the sides of the van and he secured the child in one of the cages, locked the door and backed out of the van, closing the double doors. He slapped Scott on the shoulder. His white teeth showed through the black paint on his face as he smiled.

"Let's get out of here. Well done, my friend. Well done."

* * * *

Bern's phone woke him from a sound sleep, never a good thing. "Bern here," he answered.

"*Sippe*," a tearful voice cried. "Jacob is gone!" Margo Schmidt's voice was so agonized Bern hardly recognized it. He sat bolt upright in bed, threw off the covers and began to grab clothes, dressing as he asked questions.

"When did you notice he was missing, Margo?"

"We woke to find him gone! I don't know how, *Sippe*. We never heard a thing. We went to bed and everything was fine, I went to wake him for breakfast and his bed was empty." Margo began sobbing and her husband's voice came over the phone. His voice was more bear than human.

"I will kill them, my *Sippe*. Send a hunting party. We will search."

"Can you find a scent, Alexander?"

A roar sounded on the other end of the line, full of both anger and sorrow. "No," he growled. "There is so scent, no tracks. Nothing. Like ghosts stole in the night, but I will find them. They will not get away with my son."

"No, they won't, Alexander. I will pull out all stops. I will also call in the wolves, they are the best trackers around. We will find them, but please, stay there until we arrive and set up a plan. Don't run off half-cocked."

"I will try, but hurry."

"I'm on my way."

Bern was already dressed, his next call was to Martin, he directed him to call out the all the guards in the clan. This would be an all-out assault, he would keep a skeleton crew in town to guard the population, but everyone else would be searching for Jacob Schmidt.

Next he called Sebastian Von Drake. One day after their bonding and already he was calling on their bond. They hadn't even performed the ceremony in front of Sebastian's pack yet. What a cluster fuck.

"Bastian, HUNTS hit last night. We have a missing cub." No time for greetings or small talk, Bern just laid it on the table.

If Sebastian was less than alert before the call you would never know it, he answered straight in operational mode. "I'm on my way. I'll bring my three best trackers. How many other men do you need? Do you want the whole pack? All my guards?"

Bastian felt his heart swell, with that many shifters searching they would have to be able to track the cub.

"If you could bring all the guards I would appreciate it. We should be able to cover every possible escape route between your men and mine."

"I'll make the calls now. Where do you want to meet?"

Bern gave him the address, and signed off, feeling slightly better, knowing he had the help of the best trackers in the area and double the man power to help in the search. He quickly dialed Jenna to let her know what was going on.

"Hi, darling," she answered.

"Hi, Jenna."

"What's the matter?"

"You already know me so well. One of our cubs was kidnapped last night."

"Oh my God! No! Who was it? Is it one of my students?"

"I don't know. It's Jacob Schmidt."

"Oh, I know him. He's in First grade. He's adorable. Poor little boy, he must be scared to death! His poor parents! Is there anything I can do?"

"No, little one, just keep yourself safe. Make sure you stay with Hans. Sebastian and his guards are on their way and his group and ours will be out searching as soon as we get organized."

"I can't have my phone on in class, but text me and let me know what's going on. I'll check my phone whenever I can. Please be careful."

"I will, little one. You be careful too."

"I promise. I love you."

"I love you too. I have to go."

Bern pulled into Margo and Alexander Schmidt's driveway. Alexander paced the front porch. Bern jumped from his SUV and ran toward Alex, he hugged the other man. The bear needed the support of his alpha and physical contact gave him necessary strength.

Vehicle after vehicle pulled into the driveway after Bern's arrival. The clan was assembling, it was a search party, a hunting party. Jacob Schmidt would be found.

Chapter Thirteen

The Schmidt's kitchen became a command post, the kitchen table was covered with maps. Communication devices were handed out to everyone in the search party, specially made to be used in both human and shifted forms, the two way radio bracelets were self-adjusting, regulating to the size of the arm of the wearer.

Bern divided the city and outlying areas into quadrants, two man teams would search each section. Reporting in every twenty minutes, time was of the essence. Every minute was a step farther Jacob got from home, and lessened the chance of him being found.

Sebastian arrived just as Bern was sending out the first of the search groups. His expression was grave and he spoke through their mind link.

Is it the same as with our cubs? No scent? No tracks?

Bern nodded.

My best trackers are here, but…you know they searched for our own cubs and found nothing. We will do our best, but be prepared for the worst.

Bern met his gaze. *I will not accept that. We will find Jacob. I have faith.*

I had faith too. Bastian responded.

Bern looked down at the floor for a moment, then squared his shoulders and looked back up at Sebastian. "Welcome, my friend," he said aloud. "Bring your trackers and come this way." He led them to Jacob's bedroom.

The three wolves stripped and shifted, scented the air, and then began a methodical search of the room. From corner to corner each wolf searched, scenting every object in the room, toys, bedding, and furniture.

Finally, they shifted back, standing naked, unconcerned for their state of undress, they turned to Sebastian. As one they shook their heads, and the lead wolf stated. "I'm sorry, Alpha. There is nothing here, but the scent of bears. Nothing at the window or door to the room. Nothing in the room." The wolf and his brethren looked down at the floor, embarrassed and disheartened to have disappointed their Alpha.

Sebastian laid a hand on the wolf's shoulder. "It is not your fault, Johnathon. You cannot find what is not there. Go outside search the perimeter. Do not despair. We will find Jacob, and hopefully our cubs too."

Sebastian stroked a hand through the wolf's hair and he calmed from the soothing gesture, nodded and shifted back to wolf form, the other two following suit. The three wolves padded from the room and headed toward the front of the house.

"How are they managing to leave no scent," Bern raged.

"I can only think that their scientists have somehow come up with a way to mask their scent, my friend. I do not know," Sebastian replied.

"Let's head to the campsite, maybe your trackers can pick up their scent from there," Bern said.

"Good idea. Let's go."

Sebastian grabbed the clothes his trackers had discarded and the two men gathered communication devices and headed out the front door.

As expected, they found the campsite abandoned. The only indication anyone had ever been there was the burned out remnants of the campfire. However, the scents of the HUNTS crew were strong.

They were able to easily discern the distinct identities of the five men. They would be able to identify them if they could find them. If. That was the problem. Finding them. Tracks from three vehicles left the campgrounds and they were able to follow them to the place where they had parked in the woods to kidnap Jacob, but from there it was a bust.

It looked as though each vehicle had taken off in a different direction. They were intentionally confusing the trail. The men had taken to main roads, paved roads, and there was no way to follow a trail on paved roads. No scent to follow in a vehicle, and they didn't even know which vehicle held the child. Which direction to follow. Oh, God, where did they go from here?

The sun was rising high in the sky now. It was almost noon. What time had Jacob been taken? They didn't even know that. How many hours head start did the kidnappers have? They could be a hundred miles from here by now. What direction were they travelling? There had to be a clue somewhere, Bern just had to find it.

He texted Jenna.

Campsite abandoned. Found tracks to abduction sight, but lost them from there. Search continues. Will advise. Love you.

Sebastian walked up and laid a hand on his shoulder. "We have tire tracks. Is anyone in your clan good on computers?"

"Yes, Guiles is a genius on computers. Why?"

"We might be able to determine what kind of vehicles they are driving from the tire tracks. I've seen it on those crime shows on TV."

"Brilliant! I'll get Guiles over here straight away. At least then we could be on the lookout for the cars!"

* * * *

Jenna did her best to put on a smiling happy front for the children at school. They didn't know what was going on, and weren't supposed to know. She couldn't let on that anything was wrong. She was going to deserve an Academy award for her performance today.

At lunch she checked her phone and saw the text from Bern. Not good news, but something at least. She texted back.

Praying for Jacob's safe return. Love you too.

Because of the kidnapping Hans wasn't content to guard from outside as usual, and insisted on being in the classroom with her. Jenna had worried it would disrupt the children, but they seemed to take it in stride. After the announcement this weekend, they all now knew she was the *Sippe's* mate and the extra security didn't faze them.

Though Jenna worried constantly, the afternoon passed quickly. Twenty five-year olds kept you on your toes. When afternoon pick-up started Jenna's phone rang.

"Jenna, it's Julia. I'm so sorry, but I'm over at Margo Schmidt's house. She is a basket case. Dagmar is going to come and pick up Sarah, but she's running a few minutes late."

"No problem, Julia. I'll take her out on the playground until Dagmar gets here. We'll be fine. I feel so badly for Margo. You take care of her. Are you sure you don't just want me to take Sarah home with me?"

"That's so kind of you, but no. Dagmar is already on her way. Thanks."

"Okay, I'll talk to you soon. Bye."

Sarah looked up from her seat, bless her soul and shifter hearing. "Mommy's going to be late, again!" she said.

Jenna laughed. "Well, technically, your Aunt Dagmar is going to be late," she said.

"Yeah, whatever." Sarah sighed.

"Am I so bad?" Jenna asked.

At that Sarah smiled. "No, you're terrific!"

"Okay then! As soon as everyone else is picked up, we'll go play on the swings."

"Cool!"

It only took about ten minutes for the room to clear out and leave only Jenna, Sarah and Hans. Jenna extended a hand to Sarah. "Okay, little girl, let's go!" Swinging hands, Jenna and Sarah walked ahead of Hans out to the playground.

Hans took up his usual spot on the bench and watched as Jenna pushed Sarah on the swings. "Do you want to sing a song?" Jenna asked.

"I don't know. What kind of song? I don't really know any songs?"

"How about *Five Little Monkey's Swingin' in a Tree*?" Jenna tickled her, and Sarah laughed. "Because you're a silly little monkey."

"Am not," she squealed. "I'm a big ole bear!"

Jenna stilled and stopped the swing, something was wrong, she could feel it. She turned to look at Hans and saw him slumped on the bench. "Hans!" she shouted and he didn't respond.

She grabbed Sarah and started running toward the school, whispering in her ear. "Something is wrong. If something happens to me, you get to the school. Lock yourself in my room. Hide. Stay safe." Jenna could feel the tiny body in her arms trembling.

Claws sprouted from the ends of Jenna's hands, *well that was new*. Footsteps sounded behind them, thundering closer. Senses on overload, Jenna heard something whistle through the air and then a thunk and a sharp pain in her neck, she fell to her knees, Sarah still clutched in her arms. "Run, Sarah, run," was all she managed before everything went black.

* * * *

John and Kyle chased after Jenna and Sarah, John stopped and took aim with the tranquillizer gun, he shot the dart into Jenna's neck and she dropped to her knees and then fell forward to the ground. Sarah jumped from her arms and continued running toward the school. John aimed another dart and shot the child, she fell immediately.

Kyle was already scooping the child into his arms when John reached them. Jenna was prone on the ground with her arms stretched toward them. Claws extended from the ends of her hands.

"What the hell is that?" Kyle asked. "I thought the school teacher was human? We've been watching them for weeks. She was documented as human. How the hell does she have claws?"

John walked over and examined Jenna's neck, he found the fresh bite mark. "Look at this. She has a bite mark on her neck. She must have mated with one of the bears. This could be the break through we've been looking for. The rumors may be true about shifters being able to change their mates. We'll take the teacher too. Elizabeth will be over the moon. Let's get the hell out of here."

John threw Jenna over his shoulder in a fireman's carry and the two men took off at jog for the van. Once both Jenna and Sarah were secured in cages the van began the journey toward the laboratory in the Smokey Mountains.

John was feeling very self-satisfied. Not only did they have the two bear cubs, but a shifter's mate too. He couldn't wait to dump them with Elizabeth and get the hell out of Dodge. He needed a vacation, he was taking ten days in Aruba before he headed to Arizona and the lion pride. He needed to decompress.

Three hours he drove southwest, out of the Blue Ridge Mountains in West Virginia and into the Great Smokey Mountains in North Carolina. His captives slept peacefully in their cages, never stirring. Kyle rode shotgun, splitting his attention between the rearview mirror and the inert captives in the back.

"Do you really think shifters can change people?" Kyle asked.

"I don't know," John answered. "But it certainly is something interesting to explore."

"Did you call ahead and let Dr. Montrose know we were coming?" Kyle asked.

"No, I wanted to surprise her with our little shifter mate," John said.

Kyle laughed. "How long until we get there?"

"I forgot you haven't been to the compound before. We're almost there."

Kyle looked around. "You're kidding. We're in the middle of nowhere."

"Exactly," John replied.

Kyle sat wide eyed as John drove them into the mountain. Now that they had arrived John used the intercom system to call down and have three gurneys sent up to transport their captives. Elizabeth arrived with the equipment.

John was opening the van doors when she walked up. "Why three gurneys, John? Did you bring an extra child?"

"Something better, Liz. I brought you a shifter's mate."

"What do you mean?"

"A human teacher at the school where we snatched one of the kids must have recently mated a shifter. She has a bite mark on her neck."

"You kidnapped a human! What the hell were you thinking, John! We don't harm humans!"

"Hold your horses, Liz. She was with the kid when we grabbed her and before we could tranq her she sprouted claws."

Elizabeth sputtered. "She what? Claws, let me see?"

John went to pull Jenna from her cage, but the woman was now semi-conscious. "Where am I? What do you want?" she mumbled.

John pulled her from the vehicle and placed her on one of the gurneys. Her hands were now completely normal. Jenna's head flopped from side to side and she mumbled constantly. "Sarah? Where is Sarah? Where am I?"

Dr. Montrose crossed to her and held her head in place, she looked at John. "What is her name?"

"Jenna Raynes."

"Jenna, try and clam down," the doctor said as Jenna was strapped to the gurney. "You are safe and Sarah is unharmed. Relax, rest and when you wake up I will explain it all to you. Just rest now." Elizabeth stroked her hair and Jenna closed her eyes and appeared to go back to sleep.

Elizabeth crossed to John. "What the hell have you done? You can't take humans! Humans aren't like shifters, her parents will call the police. You are a blithering idiot!"

John grabbed her by the shoulders and shook her. "You think the police are a problem? God, how can you be so naïve, when your father practically runs this program? We can do anything we want. No one will stop us. No one will question us."

* * * *

About half a dozen men were gathered around Guiles' laptop in the Schmidt's kitchen. They had determined that one of the vehicles was a Jeep Grand Cherokee, and another was a large cargo van, but they couldn't determine what make or model. The third was an SUV, with fifteen inch tires, but it appeared they all used the same type tires, so it could be any make or model.

This was getting no closer to finding Jacob. Bern started to pace the confines of the room. His patience was wearing thin. A sudden stab of terror hit him, like nothing he had ever felt in his life. He fell to his knees. *Run, Sarah, run!* Screamed through his mind and then total silence.

A broken roar swelled from his throat and rattled the windows of the house. Fur sprouted from every pore and fangs filled his mouth, his clothing split and tore. He stood, no longer human, an enraged ten foot grizzly bear tearing hell-bent for leather toward the front door and escape.

His mate, he had to get to his mate. Sebastian raced ahead of him and opened the door before he could tear it from the frame. He ran blind with rage and fear, he kept calling to Jenna in his mind and she didn't answer. Nothing. Their connection was gone. Blank. The hunters had never killed before, please God, don't let them have killed his mate.

He raced toward the center of town and eventually Sebastian's word's reached him through their mind link. *Calm down, my friend. You can still feel her life force. I can feel it through our link. She only sleeps.*

Sebastian had shifted and followed Bern in wolf form. Several others in the pack followed in SUVs. Bern took a deep breath and tried to calm his racing heart. Yes, there it was. He could feel his mate. She lived. *They were after Sarah, my niece. Oh God, Bastian. What will I tell my sister?*

One crisis at a time, my friend. Let's find your mate and determine what happened.

They reached the school and crashed through the front doors, Bern headed straight for Jenna's classroom. He shifted back to human as he reached the door, clasping the handle he threw it open and was greeted with nothing but an empty room.

Nothing was out of place, no signs of a struggle and no Jenna or Sarah. The scents of dozens of shifter and human children mingled with the scent of his mate and Hans. He followed the fresh scent of Hans and Jenna to the playground and discovered his guard, unconscious on a park bench with a tranquillizer dart still embedded in his neck.

Bern left Sebastian and the newly arrived Martin to deal with Hans while he frantically searched for Jenna. It was an open area, where the hell could she be? He shifted back to bear so he could more easily follow her scent and tracked her from the swing set along the trail back toward the school.

He found the area where she fell. He sat on his haunches in his big bear form and scratched his chest. They took her. That was the only possibility and it was their first and last mistake. Bern stood and roared again, but this time it was a roar of triumph. Victory was in their hands. HUNTS didn't know it, but they had signed their death warrants. They could mask their scents, hide their tracks, they could travel from here to Timbuktu, but they could never hide a bonded mate from a shifter.

It was true that Jenna hadn't completed her first shift yet, but Bern already held her in his heart. He knew her thoughts and her feelings and he could sense where she was from anywhere in the world. They would be able to find them now. All they had to do was pray to the God and Goddess that the HUNTS crew kept Jenna with the cubs.

Bern shifted back to human and stood panting hunched over with his hands on his knees for a few moments. Three shifts in less than an hour had him worn out. "Toss me a pair of pants," he called to Martin, and a pair of sweat pants sailed through the air in his direction.

Bern sauntered back toward the crowd gathered around the groggy, but slowly waking Hans, an injection of Yohimbine reversing the effects of the Ketamine. "They have taken Jenna," Bern said.

Sebastian looked up in shock. "Why the hell would they do that?" he asked.

"I don't know, but it's the first mistake they've made. We'll be able to track them now. Get everyone together. We need all the firepower we can get. Do you have anyone good with explosives in your pack?"

"Explosives? Are you fucking serious?" Sebastian balked.

"You bet I am. If we find their laboratory there will be nothing left of it but smoke and ashes," Bern replied in a voice as cold as ice.

"I have two men who are former Navy SEALs. One is a demolitions expert, but I don't know if he has any explosives on hand," Sebastian answered.

"I also have a demolitions expert in my clan. Former Special Forces. We have Semtex and detonators, timers, everything we will need." Bern nodded and turned striding toward one of the SUVs.

"Martin, gather the inner circle. Sebastian come with me. We will rendezvous at my home, sixteen hundred hours," Bern tossed over his shoulder never breaking stride.

Sebastian followed him, but in his mind he heard. *It is a good thing I like you, my friend. I am not used to taking orders. You would do well to remember that.*

Bern's step faltered for a moment and then he continued on, but he nodded his head in acknowledgement.

"I better call Alice," Bern said.

"I do not envy you that task, my friend," Sebastian chuckled.

Bern called as they careened out of the school parking lot, Alice answered on the first ring.

"Hey big guy, are you holding up my girl again? I thought she'd be home by now."

Bern cleared his throat. "Um, there is a small problem, Miss Alice."

"Problem? Whutz up? Your crazy sister late picking up her kid again?"

"Um, well…"

"Spit it out bear. You're makin' me nervous," Alice barked.

"Did Jenna tell you about the missing cub from last night?" Bern queried.

"No, she didn't say shit. You got my girl keepin' secrets from me, already? What the fuck is going on, bear?"

"Another cub has been taken, my niece, Sarah."

"And let me guess, Jenna was with Sarah when she was taken? Am I warm?"

"Yes, Jenna was taken too."

"Fuck a duck! I'm getting Louie!"

"Louie?"

"My Louisville Slugger, I'll kill those bastards!" Alice screamed.

"That's my mate," Sebastian whispered.

"I appreciate your sentiment, Miss Alice, but we have it under control. I assure you I will have Jenna home safe and sound by supper tonight."

"You better, bear. I'm calling her parents!" With that the line went dead.

Great. Just the way Bern wanted to meet the in-laws.

* * * *

Ten vehicles and fifty shifters set out from Bern's house less than thirty minutes later. Jenna was awake, but groggy. Bern could feel her anger and frustration. She was trying to figure out where she was and what her captors wanted.

He caught only glimpses of what she saw in his mind. A huge underground cavern, lights flickering above, white coats. Sebastian drove because Bern wanted to be able to concentrate on Jenna and any images he received from her. The words he'd heard when Sarah had been taken were the first time she had communicated telepathically with him and he didn't know if she'd be able to do it again.

Bern reached for her with his mind. *Little one, can you hear me?*

A startled gasp sounded in his head. *Oh my God, Bern, is that you? I won't tell you to get out of my head this time. How are you doing this?*

I told you we would be able to communicate telepathically once we were fully bonded.

But, I haven't shifted yet.

No, but you are obviously gifted.

He heard her laughter in his mind. *Not gifted enough. I got caught by these jag offs and they got Sarah. Bern, I'm scared.*

I know, little one. Be strong, we are on our way.

On your way? How do you know where we are? I don't even know where we are.

I can sense you. We are following your trail. Is Sarah still with you?

Yes. Sarah and Jacob are both here. We are at some kind of lab I think. Underground. The doctor was really mad that the guy brought me because I'm human. She said it would cause problems, and the guy said it wouldn't. That they had government backing.

How many people have you seen?

We are still in the parking area. Only the men who brought us, three, and four lab guys, plus the doctor. The doctor and the guy, I think his name is John, are still arguing.

Pretend to sleep, so they don't drug you again.

I'll try. They stopped talking and the doctor walked away. They are taking us somewhere.

Okay, don't try to talk now. Concentrate on breathing slowly and evenly. I know you are scared, little one, but I am coming. I promise you I will be there soon. I love you.

A feeling of warmth and love touched Bern's heart. He could feel her fear, but she was keeping it under control.

The convoy continued to head southeast, through the Blue Ridge Mountains and headed toward the Smokeys. They were only an hour or so behind the HUNTS crew and should be nearing their location soon. Bern could sense himself coming closer to his mate and his heart soared.

Soon he would once again hold her in his arms. After he slaughtered the men who had dared to touch what was his.

Bern are you there? Jenna's soft voice touched his mind, wiping the anger away.

Yes, my sweet. What's going on?

I think I'm going to be sick. I'm in a cage! They took us in an elevator, down I think, to a laboratory. Bern—Jenna's voice cracked. *There are dozens of children here. I can't see all the cages, so I can't count how many exactly, but my God, Bern, there are so many. Will we be able to rescue them all?*

We will, my sweet. We will not leave one shifter child behind. "Damn, Jenna says there are dozens of shifter children in cages in a lab at the facility," Bern relayed to Sebastian.

Sebastian's eyes lit with hope. "My cubs may be there then."

"That's true, but how will we transport all those children?"

"Once we get them out and to safety I can call in a helicopter to transport them out."

"You have a helicopter?"

"Yes."

"Well. You're just full of surprises," Bern said.

Sebastian just smiled and then relayed the information that their pack cubs were most likely in the lab facility to his pack members. Several growls came over the radios in response to the news. Good. Bern was glad the wolves were as invested in vengeance as he was.

"Stop here," Bern said.

All the vehicles pulled off the road and the shifters exited en mass. They formed a circle around Bern. "The compound is in that direction," Bern said pointing to the west. "We need to shift into our animal forms and scout the area. Jenna said they were being held underground. Look for an entrance to an underground facility. Watch for cameras, booby traps, electronic surveillance. Our biggest advantage is surprise. They don't know we're coming. We can't tip them off that we're here. Make sure that you are not seen. Meet back here in one hour."

The men split up, hid the vehicles in the trees, stripped and shifted. Wolves and bears slipped quietly into the forest and disappeared. Bern and Bastian travelled together, a golden bear and black wolf. Though Bern was a very large bear he moved soundlessly through the woods, his light fur blending with the fall leaves and trees. The black wolf kept to the shadows, a shadow himself, darkness personified.

Bern was drawn to the entrance of the mountain, but it was tricky getting there without being seen by the many cameras posted along the way. They made their way around and above the cameras, climbing up the steep incline and coming at the entrance from above.

They would have to blow the entrance, and once they did the HUNTS crew would know they were coming. How many men were inside? And would they be able to get to the hostages before they had a chance to kill them? Would they kill them to keep them from being rescued?

Jenna, how many people are in the lab area?

The four men who brought us down, the doctor and four guards that I can see at each of the exits.

Have you seen any other guards?

No, but I've only seen this room.

What happened to the men who brought you?

I don't know. I think they left, but I'm not sure.

Okay, little one. We are here. We're going to be coming in soon. Be ready. Is there any way you can warn the children?

All the children are sedated. Jenna's voice hiccupped a sob. *They are hooked up to IV's and out cold. Bern, what are they doing to them?*

I don't know, baby? Have they done anything to you?

No, and they know I'm awake. The doctor just looks at me and shakes her head.

Okay, don't do anything to draw attention to yourself. We'll be there soon.

Okay, I love you.

Love you too.

Bern nodded to Bastian and they began to make their way back to the rendezvous point.

* * * *

Jenna sat on the cot in her cage and twisted her hands together. Two weeks ago she was nothing but a kindergarten teacher in a shifter town. Now she *was* a shifter. Well, almost a shifter, mated, kidnapped and in a freakin' cage. What the fuck?

The doctor walked over to Jenna's cage and Jenna looked at the floor. Oh shit, what now. "I'm sorry you have been caught up in this, miss…"

Should she answer? "Jenna, Jenna Raynes."

"Miss Raynes. I am Dr. Elizabeth Montrose."

"Why are you doing this?" Jenna asked. "These are children. Don't you understand you are taking them from their families? What are you doing to them?"

The doctor flushed. "I am not harming them. Only testing their blood. It is necessary for the greater good. To find a cure for the diseases that decimate the human population; cancer, AIDS, ALS, MS, and others."

"You are harming them. Look at them! They are unconscious. In cages. Scared, alone, away from their families. How can you justify what you are doing?"

"Their blood could save millions!"

"There are other ways. You could have asked for donations. Asked the shifters for blood samples."

"You don't think we tried that?" the doctor screamed. "We asked, we cajoled, we begged. They all refused. They can heal, they never get sick, they live for hundreds of years and yet they refuse to share the secrets of their health with the human race."

"I'm sorry, but that is still their right. It doesn't give you the right to take what isn't yours."

Dr. Montrose turned her back and paced across the floor. She rested her hands on a metal table and bowed her head for a moment then turned and paced back. She stopped at the bars of the cage and met Jenna's gaze, her look was hard and cold.

"When it is your life that is in jeopardy see what decision you would make," she spat and turned on her heal and marched out of the room.

Jenna stared at her clasped hands, what the hell did that mean? Dr. Montrose was a piece of work, trying to justify kidnapping children because she was going to save the world from disease. No. Sorry. It didn't fly in Jenna's book.

One of the white coated technicians entered the cage where Sarah was lying and Jenna stood and walked to the bars of her cage. "What are you doing?" she yelled. "Don't you hurt her!"

The man looked over his shoulder at her and shook his head. "Shut up or I'll sedate you too," he barked, dismissing her. He inserted a needle in Sarah's arm and withdrew a blood sample, filling three separate vacuum tubes, before exiting the cubicle. He sneered in Jenna's direction as he stepped to a counter, labeled the samples and placed them in a refrigerated unit. The disdain in his face was clear, she was beneath him, less than human. A lab rat, nothing more.

Dr. Montrose returned through a door at the back left of the lab, speaking briefly with the guard at the door. She walked right up to Jenna, who still stood at the bars of her cage. "I'm sorry I lost my temper. It's a fault of mine. I am passionate about my research," she said.

Jenna took a deep breath, antagonizing her captors would not get her anywhere. "I understand. We will just have to agree to disagree."

"Would you allow me to take your blood?" Dr. Montrose asked.

Oh shit! What should she do? If she said no they would most likely sedate her and take it anyway, and then she wouldn't be able to help Bern when they came to rescue the children. They would destroy the lab when they came, so the blood would never be tested, right? Okay, let them take it.

"Why would you want my blood? As you said I am only a human," Jenna stalled.

Dr. Montrose arched a brow at her. "I think we both know you are more than that, now don't we? John said you sprouted claws and roared when they tried to take the bear cub from you. Can you explain how that happened?"

Jenna faked a laugh. "I think your man must be on drugs. I may have roared in anger, as I think anyone would do if a loved one was being pried from their arms, but my only claws are these." She flashed Dr. Montrose her manicured nails.

"Why is it I doubt your veracity?" the doctor asked.

Jenna shrugged her shoulders. "Maybe you've been hanging around the wrong group of people," she said scanning the room with a vicious gaze.

"Touché," Dr. Montrose replied. "However, you still haven't answered my question. Will you allow me to take your blood? It was your suggestion that I ask instead of take."

"Hoist by my own petard. So it was, good doctor. Yes, I will allow you take my blood."

"Please go and sit on the cot."

Jenna complied and the doctor retrieved a tourniquet, syringe and several vacuum tubes from a nearby drawer. When she returned one of the guards accompanied her. She unlocked the cage and the guard entered first.

"Do not move from the cot or make any sudden movements." The guard stood to Jenna's left while the doctor took up a position to her right. "Extend your right arm please."

Jenna hated needles and doing this in a cage with a guard standing next to her was really amping up her fear factor.

Bern reached out to her. *What is it little one? I feel your fear.*

Just being stupid, they are taking my blood. I hate needles.

Bern's growl reached her mind and she almost smiled. *They will suffer for hurting you, my sweet.*

You are such a bear. I can't talk now. Ouch! The needle sank into her arm and Jenna grimaced and looked at the ceiling and counted to twenty, it would be over soon. She felt Dr. Montrose switching the vials with a pinch and swore softly.

"I'm sorry, almost through," Dr. Montrose said.

One more pinch as the vials changed and Jenna groaned, the guard stepped closer and Jenna cringed.

"Stand down, David, she just doesn't like needles. She's not going to attack me for God's sake."

"You don't know that," the guard grunted.

"She's human," Dr. Montrose said.

"Or not," the guard replied.

Dr. Montrose stuck the last vial in her lab coat pocket and removed the tourniquet, she swabbed the spot with an alcohol wipe and covered it with a small Band-Aid, patting Jenna's arm. "Thank you, Miss Raynes. I appreciate your cooperation."

"What's a little blood among friends," Jenna quipped.

We're about to blow the entrance Jenna, brace for an explosion.

Holy shit. Okay, standing by.

Dr. Montrose and the guard, David stepped from the cage and locked the door behind them just as the explosion rocked the entire building. Plaster fell from the ceiling, light fixtures exploded and swung loose from there attachments glass shattered from cabinets all over the laboratory and the technicians and guards ran like rats in a maze.

It wasn't completely dark in the laboratory, emergency lighting came on over the exits giving the space an eerie red glow. The guards began barking orders. "Get to your lock down positions."

"Secure the prisoners."

The white coated personnel all exited out a back door and a dozen or more guards flooded in from other doors.

Jenna called to Bern. *There are about sixteen guards in the laboratory now. All the technicians and the doctor have left for somewhere else.*

Thanks, we're on our way.

* * * *

The entrance blew with a mighty blast of rock and debris and the group rushed in, half in human form and half shifted. They were better fighters in their beast forms, but there were some things only a man could do, like open doors and push buttons.

Over the stench of smoke and Primacord Bern smelled a scent that enraged his bear. The man who had taken Jenna was here. Bern scanned what looked like nothing more than a parking lot, though many of the vehicles now lay on their sides or crushed by fallen debris. His nose led him to the one he was looking for in no time.

A white panel van rested no more than a hundred meters from two sets of elevator doors in the center of the structure. Undamaged, of course. As his men swarmed into the building, seeking cover among the overturned vehicles and structural supports the shots began to ring out.

Bern didn't run for cover, he charged straight ahead toward the van. That man, John, would be his. He would bathe in his blood for having touched his mate. A bullet grazed his shoulder and a solid hundred and fifty pounds of wolf knocked into his legs, right at the knees, he fell to all fours and a bullet soared over his head.

Bern growled and snapped at the wolf by his side. *You're welcome, stupid*, Bastian snarled in his head. Guards began spilling into the parking garage from hidden passages surrounding them, automatic weapons firing. But they were as good as dead. The Wolves and Bears attacked, paws the size of dinner plates with six inch claws slashed across the jugular veins of the guards before they could draw a breath.

Jaws full of razor sharp teeth clamped onto throats and squeezed or simply tore out and life ended. The walls were painted with blood and while a few shots connected with the shifters, they healed quickly, and unless you managed to hit their heart or their brain they weren't going to die.

The whole fight lasted less than five minutes and at the end twenty guards lay dead on the ground with only minor injuries to the shifters. As Bern was dispatching the last guard an engine roared to life.

He lifted his muzzle to see the white van shift into gear and careen toward the exit of the mountain. Bern roared and lumbered after the vehicle, but Sebastian's voice stopped him. *We need to find Jenna and Sarah and the cubs. There will be time enough later for vengeance.*

Bern nodded his big shaggy head. *True enough, my friend. Let's find our kin.*

Martin appeared at Bern's side in human form. "We have tracked the routes the guards used to come to the surface. There are only people on two other levels. The laboratory, which contains sixteen guards and all the captives, I scented twenty-five; and a residence level, where the staff must live. They've made it easy on us, they're all gathered in one room, five guards manning the doors. What do you want us to do with the researchers?"

Bern couldn't answer Martin in bear form so he shifted back. He addressed Bastian. *What do you think? Do we kill the researchers, capture and question them? Let them go?*

We need to question at least the doctor. I want to know how much they've learned and what it is they really want. As for the rest... It is a tough call. If they are zealots like the rest of HUNTS they are better off dead, if they are merely working for a paycheck, eh then let them go, but how do we know?

"We need the doctor for questioning. If you can safely capture and contain the others, do so. If not, eliminate at your discretion. You take Guiles, Hans, Victor, Ivan and three others of your choice and secure the residence level. Rendezvous in the clearing outside at twenty-one hundred hours," Bern said.

Martin nodded solemnly. "I understand, *Sippe*."

Bern turned to Bastian and gazed down at the black wolf. "You ready to go bite some more heads off?"

Bastian yipped at him, snapping his jaws a little too near Bern's manly treasure. "Hey! Watch it! I still want cubs you know." If a wolf could smile Bern was sure Sebastian was smiling.

As with the fight in the parking garage, the infiltration of the laboratory was over in minutes. There were a few more bullet holes on the shifter side, because they had limited access into the lab, having to enter through doorways, which made them targets for uncomfortable moments, but they entered in twos, bear and wolf, high and low, and took the guards down fast and furious.

When all the bloodshed had ended Bern found his mate huddled in the corner of her cage in a fetal ball, he approached her slowly, afraid she would fear him after seeing his animal unleashed. His sweet mate was not used to violence and anger.

He had once again shifted back to human form and prayed he didn't have to shift again for a week. His body shook with fatigue and left over adrenaline. He crouched beside her huddled form and extended his hand, stroking her hair.

She flinched and Bern's heart broke in two. "Jenna, little one," he said in a voice choked with tears.

She looked up with unfocused eyes, glazed with fear and blinked. He stroked her hair again, and grazed her cheek, smiling softly. "Little one? Are you okay? Did they hurt you?"

She blinked again and her eyes finally seemed to focus. "Bern?" she asked hesitantly, she blinked again and then shouted. "My Bern, my bear!" and threw herself into his arm so forcefully he barely managed to remain on his feet.

Now, that was more like it! His mate was in his arms, kissing the stuffing out of him. Jenna placed kisses everywhere she could reach. Kissing his forehead, cheeks, neck, and finally landing on his mouth where he deepened the kiss and explored her mouth with the passion he'd been holding back. He crushed her in his arms, standing to his feet and cradling her body as close as he could.

When he finally pulled back she said. "Oh my goodness Bern, you're naked!"

Bern threw his head back and laughed. After the day he'd had it felt really good to have something to laugh about. "Glad you noticed, baby."

"You better get some clothes on, because…um, something is…poking."

"Somebody toss me some pants," Bern yelled, and a pair of sweats sailed his way. He pulled them on and bowed to her. "Better, my lady."

She cleared her throat. "Yes, well, um."

He nuzzled her neck. "You are better than honey, little one," he said.

"Sweet talker." She laughed, then looked around the room. "We better get the kids out of here and wake them up," she said.

"That's my mate," he said. "Always thinking of the clan first. I'm so proud of you." He kissed her soundly on the lips. "You heard the lady. Let's get these kids out of here!"

Jenna went straight to Sarah's cage and unhooked her from the IV, but when she would have lifted the child into her arms, Bern took her instead. By the time they reached the upper level and exited outside darkness had fallen.

Sebastian's troops had arrived and not one, but two helicopters sat waiting in the clearing, along with medical personnel, blankets, food, water and anything else they could possibly need. That man was pretty fucking amazing.

Sarah began to wake up and murmur. "Momma, where's Momma?"

Jenna leaned over and stroked her cheek. "You'll be with Momma soon, baby girl."

Sarah blinked and looked up into Bern's face. "Unca Bern? What are you doing here?"

"Carrying you, silly girl. What does it look like?"

Sarah snuggled closer and closed her eyes again, knowing now she was safe in her uncle's arms.

Chapter Fourteen

Pandemonium exploded when the entourage arrived back at Bern's house. Sebastian had phoned ahead to let them know they were coming so everyone was there. The entire Honey Corner's Clan, all four hundred of them. The Von Drake Pack, and there must have been close to five hundred in the pack. Alice. Jenna's parent's had flown in from Nashville, how they'd managed to get a flight on such short notice she'd never know, but they were all there.

All that was missing was the Dallas Cowboy's Cheerleaders and it would have been a real party. The minute Jenna walked in the door Alice confronted her, hands on her hips she gave Jenna her best glare. "What the hell do you think you're doing going and getting yourself kidnapped? You almost gave me apoplexy!"

"Well, excuse me Queen of the World. I'm so sorry I inconvenienced you!"

Bern stood behind Jenna and watched the two yell at each other like he was watching a tennis match.

"I am so mad at you! You could have gotten hurt or even killed! That's not allowed!" Alice screamed.

"I know, sweetie. I'm sorry," Jenna said.

Then Alice collapsed into tears and threw her arms around Jenna sobbing. Mrs. Raynes walked up behind them and smiled at Bern. He looked at her and asked. "What the hell was all that about?"

"Girl code." She shrugged.

"More of that crap? I'm never going to understand girl code am I?" he asked.

"I doubt it, dear," she said patting his cheek. "Jenna, darling, do you suppose you could let go of Alice long enough to hug your mother?" she asked with the cutest southern lilt to her voice.

Jenna laughed and released Alice to hug her mother. "Oh Momma, It's so good to see ya."

Bern had to laugh. All of a sudden his little one had a southern accent. Where the hell had that come from?

A balding man in jeans and checkered shirt entered the room. Bern knew in a sniff it was Jenna's father. The man's serious eyes looked him up and down.

Then he scanned his daughter from head to toe. He looked back to Bern and nodded once, stepping closer. "She looks in one piece," he murmured. "That's a good thing for you."

Bern arched a brow at Barton Raynes. "Yes, it is, because I would kill whomever harmed a hair on her head."

"And I would kill you if a hair on her head were harmed," Barton Raynes said as smooth as silk.

Bern slapped his huge arm around the smaller man's shoulders. "I think I like you already, Mr. Raynes."

Barton looked up into Bern's face. "I just might like you too, boy." The man laughed, he turned to his daughter and opened his arms. "You got a hug for Daddy there, little girl?"

"Daddy!" Jenna squealed and launched herself at her father and hugged Bern at the same time. When she finally let go of her dad, she stepped back and grabbed her mother's hand, pulling her up beside her. "Bern, this is my mother, Cassandra and I guess you've met my dad."

"In a way." Bern laughed, he lifted Cassandra's tiny hand to his mouth and kissed her knuckles. "Pleasure to meet you, ma'am. I can see where my Jenna got her good looks."

"Oh, he is a sweet talker, Jenna, isn't he? Maybe he could teach your father a thing or two?" Cassandra teased.

"Now, Kiki, Don't be like that," Barton groused.

Jenna laughed and hooked her arm through Bern's. "Let's go sit down. I'm tired and hungry. I need food!"

Kiki laughed. "There is enough food in that kitchen to feed both the Rebels and the Yanks, so I think you're safe, little girl."

"That's one thing I'll say for these bears," Jenna said. "They know how to eat!"

They went into the kitchen, filled some plates, and then headed for Bern's office and a little peace and quiet. The five of them sequestered themselves in the office and Bern and Jenna filled Alice and her parents in on everything that had happened.

After they had evacuated all the children, Bern and his men had blown the research facility to kingdom come. HUNTS would not be utilizing that location again, it was nothing but a pile of rocks.

Now they needed to locate the packs, prides, dens, etc. that the missing children came from and return them as soon as possible. There would be some joyous reunions in the future for the shifter community.

Bern's cell phone rang and he stepped to the side of the room to answer it. "Bern here."

"It's Martin. We have the research personnel secured on the lower level of the clan house. Five technicians and the doctor." Martin growled.

"What is it?" Bern asked.

"Something I need to discuss with you in person." Martin replied.

"Do you want to come up now?"

"No, tomorrow is soon enough," Martin said with a sigh.

"I'm not going to like it, am I?"

"Probably not. I sure don't," Martin said.

"Okay, in that case, definitely keep it for tomorrow. I've had all the bad news I can take for today."

"Roger that. I'll see you in the morning for briefing," Martin said.

"Not too early," Bern said. "It's been a hell of a day. Let's sleep in, make it nine o'clock."

"You got it, *Sippe. Guten nacht.*"

"*Guten nacht*, Martin."

Bern sat back down and pulled Jenna into his lap. "Something wrong?" she whispered.

He shrugged. "Maybe, but nothing that can't wait until morning, so not too bad."

She rested her head on his chest and her eyes drifted closed.

Kiki looked at her daughter and then her husband. "I think that's our cue to retire for the evening, Bart, Jenna is tired. Let's head up to bed and let these children get some sleep."

Jenna stirred. "I'm okay, Momma."

"You're tired as an old mule after plowing the back forty. Now don't go givin' your momma a hard time, little girl," Kiki said.

Jenna smiled up at her and nodded. "Yes, ma'am."

Kiki rose to her feet and Barton stood beside her. "Your sister, Dagmar, showed us to a lovely room in the east wing. I hope that's all right?" Kiki asked.

Bern stood with Jenna in his arms. "Of course, it's fine. I'm so glad you're here." He kissed Kiki on the cheek and nodded to Barton. Alice stood too. "Are you staying here tonight, Al?"

"No, I'm gonna head back to Jenna's, just had to make sure my girl was okay," she said.

She walked over and kissed Jenna's cheek and Bern leaned down so she could kiss his too. She exchanged goodbyes with Jenna's parents, and they left the room heading in different directions.

Once Jenna's parents were out of ear shot Bern said. "You can stop playing possum now, they're gone."

Jenna flashed a cheeky smile at him and wet her lips. "How did you know I was faking?"

"Shifter nose, little one. I can smell your desire."

She giggled. "You don't think they knew, do you?"

"No, I think they bought it," he said.

She nuzzled into his neck and began kissing up his jawline. "Mmm, good, because I need you, my bear."

"I need you too, little one. Bless my sister for putting your folks at the other end of the house."

"Smart cookie, that sister of yours"

"Mmm," was all he managed and the door to the bedroom fell shut behind them. He let her slide slowly down his body, and his already swollen cock notched into the juncture of her thighs. He slid his hands under the edge of her shirt and lifted it up and over her head in one motion, letting it drop to the floor, and backed her toward the bed.

Bern sealed his lips over hers and never severed the kiss as they moved closer and closer to the bed. Jenna kicked off her shoes. Bern stepped out of his, and unbuckled his pants, dropping them and leaving them behind on the floor in one fell swoop.

When the back of Jenna's legs reached the bed he pushed her down and pulled off his shirt in one motion. She shimmied out of her skirt and dropped it over the side of the bed before Bern settled between her open thighs.

"My sweet Jenna," he whispered. "You smell so good." He kissed down her neck to her collarbone and then across to her breastbone. His large hands cupped her breasts, and he circled her nipples with his thumbs, feeling them pucker under his attentions.

His mouth followed his hands, sucking first one and then the other turgid peak into his mouth and releasing them with a soft pop. He licked around her areola and then blew softly across the peaks, watching goose bumps appear on Jenna's skin.

Her soft round belly called to him and he kissed the mound, pausing at her navel to lave the little dimple. Jenna giggled. "Are you ticklish?" he asked.

"Yes." She squirmed and he dug his fingers into her sides and tickled until she was rolling on the bed trying to get away from him, laughing and squealing. He slipped his hands behind her back, palmed her ass, and pressed his face into her stomach laughing.

"I'm sorry, little one, but I couldn't help myself. I love to hear you laugh."

She leaned up on her elbows and stared down at him, her eyes glowing with love and laughter. He rested his chin on her pelvic bone and stared up at her. "You better make it up to me," she teased.

He pulled his head back a tiny bit and teased her clit with the tip of his tongue. "Like that?"

She threw her head back and moaned. "Mmm, good start."

Never one to turn down a challenge Bern began to lick and suck her in earnest. Teasing the moist entrance to her sex with a finger, he traced the seam up and down. Jenna squirmed trying to force his hand and make him penetrate her, but Bern would not be rushed.

Her honey was abundant, covering the lips of her sex, he coated his fingers and drew the lubrication to the puckered rosette of her anus. Jenna gasped, but didn't pull away. He sucked her clit into his mouth as he thrust one finger into her ass knuckle deep.

He lifted his mouth for a moment and murmured. "Okay?"

"Yes, yes," she panted.

He moved, sliding the finger in and out, working the lubrication inside her while teasing her clit mercilessly. "I'm going to add a second finger, push out as I push in, little one."

"Okay," she breathed.

He pushed in and he felt her quiver and stiffen for a moment. "Relax, breathe, it's okay."

"Hurts," she panted.

"I can stop."

"No, it's okay now. Just feel so full."

"Think how full you'll feel when it's my cock that's in your tight little ass," Bern said. His cock was a slab of marble just thinking about it.

Jenna shivered and a fresh burst of honey dripped from her pussy, obviously she liked that idea too. Bern worked his fingers, scissoring them inside her, stretching her tissues and preparing her to take his cock.

He licked in circles around her clit, the little bundle of nerves peeking out of its hood and begging for attention. She was close to climaxing, but Bern didn't want her to come alone, he wanted to be balls deep in her when she climaxed, gripping his cock like a vise.

He pulled his fingers free and Jenna cried out in distress. "Get on your knees for me, little one." He reached into his night stand and grabbed the bottle of lube, liberally coating his dick and pressing more in and around her rosette.

Lining up behind her he pressed his throbbing hard on to the entrance of her forbidden hole. "Put your head and shoulders down on the bed, baby and push out for me."

He reached under her body with one arm, securing her around the waist and held his cock with his other hand slowly pressing forward, the head of his dick passed the first ring of muscles and he bit his cheek to keep from blowing his load like a fifteen-year-old.

"You are so fucking tight, it's like a vise gripping my cock."

"Oh fuck, fuck, you're gonna make me come. You know how it turns me on when you talk dirty to me."

Bern grunted and kept pressing forward until he was finally fully seated inside her, balls tight against her creaming pussy. "I could come just from looking at this picture. You have the best ass in the world, and I'm inside it."

Jenna moaned.

"Gotta move now, little one," Bern said, and he slowly pulled back and thrust forward. He reached around and played with her pussy, thrusting two fingers inside her and pressing his thumb to her clit.

Jenna was thrusting back at him and he began to pound into her harder and harder. The bed was rocking, the headboard banging against the wall, Jenna was keening. He could feel her pussy clamping down on his fingers. He was about to lose it.

"Come for me, Jenna," he cried and he circled her clit with his thumb and thrust hard into her tight ass, he pressed down hard on her nub and she cried out, her pussy and her ass clamping down on him.

Bern grabbed her hips and pounded into her like a man possessed, three thrusts and then he held himself deep inside her emptying his seed and climaxing so hard stars burst behind his closed eyelids.

He collapsed over her back, careful to keep his weight on his arms, and kissed the curve of her spine, her neck, she turned her head and reached for a kiss. She fell from her knees and his softening erection slipped from her ass. She rolled to her side and Bern flopped down beside her, taking her in his arms.

"Oh my God, Bern, that was amazing," Jenna said.

"You're amazing."

They cuddled for a few minutes with her head on her shoulder and then Bern said. "Since your folks are already here, why don't we get married tomorrow?"

"Tomorrow? Are you crazy? How do we plan a wedding in one day?"

"Jenna, this is Honey Corners. We know how to throw a party."

She sat up in bed and looked at him. "Well hell... Why not?"

Epilogue

Martin paced in front of the cages in the basement of his *Sippe Leiter's* house as he had for the last three hours and paused once again in front of Dr. Elizabeth Montrose's cell. It was midnight and the woman was sleeping.

She was five-foot three-inches of devastation to his six-foot five-inch frame. She was human. She was sick. Leukemia if his nose was correct. She was the enemy. And she was his mate. Fuck!

The End

About the Author

Tamara Hoffa lives in central Tennessee, with her husband of 30 years, her parents, 2 dogs and 2 cats. She started reading at four years old and has rarely been seen without a book since. At home you will usually find her in "nana's chair" with her kindle, her laptop or one of her precious, precocious grandson's in her lap. Tamara is an author, an editor, and reviews/promotions coordinator for Secret Cravings Publishing. Tamara is proof positive that it's never too late to reach for your dreams.

Find me at:
Website: http://www.tamarahoffa.com

Facebook : https://www.facebook.com/AuthorTamaraHoffa

Twitter: https://www.twitter.com/TamaraHoffa

Goodreads:
http://www.goodreads.com/author/show/6537898.Tamara_Hoffa

Blog: http://sslyblog.wordpress.com/

Pinterest http://www.pinterest.com/tamarahoffa/
Amazon:http://www.amazon.com/Tamara-Hoffa/e/B009FG9PCE/ref=sr_ntt_srch_lnk_1?qid=1398090026&sr=1-1
Goggle +
https://plus.google.com/u/0/100155539737780435355/posts

Other books by Tamara
Roping Love
Chasing Love
Fetching Love
A Special Kind of Love

Coming soon – Book 2 in the Animal in Me series- Bear Blood!

Prologue- 1994

Pale and weak, the child lay on the stark white sheets of the big bed that made her look so tiny. The khaki colored U.S. Army ball cap that rested on her head enhanced the sallow tone of her skin, but Lizzy never took that cap off. Daddy gave it to her, and she was Daddy's girl. He said it would make her strong, like him. She needed to be strong, because she felt so weak.

Her big brown eyes scanned the room she had been confined to for the last two weeks. Nothing had changed. She was so tired. Tubes in her nose, I.V. in her arm, pain everywhere. Where were Mommy and Daddy? One of them was usually in the chair by her bed when she woke up. It didn't matter, she couldn't keep her eyes open much longer anyway. She'd go back to sleep and they'd be there when she woke up. Well, if she woke up. She heard the doctor's talking, and she knew the truth: she might die soon.

It wasn't so bad. If she died she would live with the angels and all the pain would stop. But, Daddy kept saying she had to fight, and mommy would cry…

Secret Cravings Publishing
www.secretcravingspublishing.com

Made in the USA
Charleston, SC
19 March 2015